RED MUTINY

John Wingate

SAPERE
BOOKS

RED MUTINY

Published by Sapere Books.

20 Windermere Drive, Leeds, England, LS17 7UZ,
United Kingdom

saperebooks.com

ISBN: 978-1-80055-641-6

Good friends, sweet friends, let me not stir you up
To such a sudden flood of mutiny.
— *Julius Caesar*, William Shakespeare

RANKS AND RATES

Royal Navy Officers:
Admiral
Vice Admiral
Rear Admiral
Commodore
Captain
Commander
Lieutenant-Commander
Lieutenant
Sub-Lieutenant
Acting/Sub-Lieutenant

Soviet Navy Officers:
Admiral
Vitse-Admiral
Kontr-Admiral
Kapitan Pervogo Ranga
Kapitan Vtorogo Ranga
Kapitan Tretyego Ranga
Kapitan Leytenant
Starshiy Leytenant
Leytenant
Mladshiy Leytenant

Royal Navy Ratings:
Chief Petty Officer: CPO
Petty Officer: PO
Chief Radio Electrical Artificer: CREA
Chief Marine Engineering Artificer: CMEA

Marine Engineering Artificer: MEA
Able Seaman: AB
Radio Operator: RO
Marine Engineering Mechanic: MEM

COLLATOR'S INTRODUCTION

No, I have no regrets. I am relaxing in the comfort of the Inter-City Express to Liverpool and am watching the serene fields of the Northampton uplands rolling past the window. After a month's leave, I am rejoining the company's newest container ship, *Timor Princess*, to take her out to New Zealand via Boston and Panama. Captain Derek Warne, Extra Master, now — but it was very different then, when I was third mate of *Eastern Princess*. She was running general cargo from Auckland to Buenos Aires, via the Cape, Durban and Australia.

No regrets? Almost true... All will depend upon whether we have succeeded with the timing. Less than an hour and a half ago, I delivered personally the typed manuscript to the publishers. It was their insistence and encouragement which finally overcame my reluctance to offer the manuscript. These tormented pages from the unknown — unexpurgated as I found them — will best tell their own story without further comment from me.

I was not proud of my action at the time. The longer I procrastinated, the more difficult it was to decide whether to offer these pages for publication or to destroy them. I knew then that, not only was I shielding myself from an action of which I was ashamed, but that the longer I delayed, the better chance the principal actors had of safely reshaping their new lives. *Publish and be damned*, they say. Easy enough to echo, if the circumstances were not so tragic. When others' lives hang in the balance, perhaps it is better to do nothing ... but it is too late now. The die is cast.

I am indebted to all those who have helped me in my research, in particular the witnesses who willingly recorded their recollections for me. I am also very grateful to the Lazarevs for their permission to publish sundry letters which I have inserted in the appropriate chapters.

PROLOGUE

Eastern Princess was a happy ship and I, Third Officer Derek Warne, was third mate. I was twenty-four, not particularly ambitious, my career following the normal pattern. Life in the ship was strict in comparison with the way things are today, but we were a disciplined and happy lot, serving under a good, if sometimes awkward, master.

As far as I remember, we discharged at Buenos Aires during the last week in December. There had been a longshoremen's strike which had held us up for a week, and the captain's temper was at fission point. He was anxious to sail as soon as we had loaded (mixed cargo, I think it was) because he had not yet seen his new daughter, who had been born in Wales on the day we sailed from Durban.

It had been a hot summer, and most of us were suffering from prickly heat. Even though we were on the homeward leg, tempers were becoming frayed, due principally to the cussedness of the Old Man. We were eight days out and had already begun to forget the low-lying coastline which we had left below the horizon astern of us. We had seen enough of the South American continent, and the green fields of England were calling.

I had the afternoon watch, the twelve-to-four, and was trying to stave off the sleepiness that afflicted us in this heat — and after the chief steward's best lunch of the week. I was pacing slowly from one side of the bridge to the other, bored beyond words, my mind blank. The radar showed nothing, the last ship having passed astern of us, Buenos Aires bound, over an hour previously. The helmsman had his head down in the corner of the bridge and the ship, dipping rhythmically into the long swell, was on 'George', the autopilot. The horizon shimmered with heat, and it was difficult to distinguish it from the glassy sea.

I was alerted from my lethargy by a sudden crack, like the report from a naval gun. I looked to starboard and was just in time to see one of those diamond-shaped ray fish, over thirty feet across, slap down in a curtain of spray upon the surface of the sea. According to the master, the ray fish rid themselves of lice in this dramatic manner, but it is rare to catch one in the act of delousing itself.

I seized the bridge binoculars to try and watch the monster beneath the surface, but it had vanished, leaving only a tell-tale stream of bubbles. I continued to search the area, when the top of my lenses cut momentarily across the indistinct horizon. I thought at first that there was dust in the eyepiece, but as I cut back along the horizon, there it was again: a small, dark speck lunging gently in the Atlantic swell. It would pass about three miles to starboard, nearer than I first thought. It was probably a detergent drum, ditched by a passing tanker. I idly took another look.

My eyes by now had become accustomed to the glare, so I refocused the binoculars to suit my vision. The dark object became sharper — and then I identified the stern-on silhouette of a small boat. Her transom was canoe-shaped and as the smudge glided abeam, it grew rapidly into the outline of a grey, Norwegian-type, aluminium whale boat, her prow pointed and with a considerable flare. While the boat rolled to the swell, I tried to see what was inboard.

I can admit now that I came up with a round-turn as I identified the shapeless, twisted bundle lying across the thwarts. I had never seen a corpse and I suppose I can be forgiven for the shameful alternatives that flashed through my mind. If *Eastern Princess* held to her course, the boat would be astern in a few minutes and no one would be the wiser. To drag the Old Man unnecessarily from his bunk at this time of the afternoon was inviting homicide. I peered again: that *was* a human being, I was sure of it. I crossed to the master's phone and, risking purgatory, informed him that I was altering towards to investigate.

I can still remember the sardonic amusement in the Old Man's eyes as he ordered me away in the starboard lifeboat — a sort of revenge, I suppose, for interrupting his afternoon's caulk.

Eastern Princess's engine throbbed astern. As the ship wallowed in the swell, the watch-on-deck slipped the disengaging gear, and then the lifeboat was chugging across to the tiny boat bobbing in utter solitude in the middle of the Atlantic. As the distance narrowed, my fears were quickly confirmed — a body lay sprawled across the thwarts.

I circled the grey dory and was surprised that her name and port of registry had been chipped off and the patch painted over. She was of metal — aluminium, I think — but, in spite of her Norwegian lines, there was something not quite right about her. I took our cutter alongside and ordered the bowman to hold on. There was no ugly rush by my boat's crew, so I boarded the vessel myself. The metal burnt my hands as I scrambled over the gunwales.

The poor devil lay face down. What was left of his shirt was in tatters; his skin was black and blistered. I hesitated, steeling myself for the horror. I had read wartime books about survivors' sufferings during the Battle of the Atlantic, and I did not relish having to face reality. I told the bowman to shove off. Then I was on my own while the cutter lay off, her engine exhaust coughing in the swell. I took hold of the shapeless thing and gingerly tried to roll it over onto its back.

I had expected *rigor mortis* and was prepared for the natural revulsion. But I cried out as I felt the warmth of the flesh when my fingers touched his chest. The blood still coursed and, though the face was puffy and there were bruises about his throat, the miracle of life still flickered in him. I shouted to the cutter and, as it bumped alongside, we gently heaved the unconscious survivor across the gunwales. While the crew tried to settle him comfortably, I took a hurried look around the mysterious craft.

There was little in the boat, save the normal survival gear. Only three oars, which was strange, and one of them broken. The built-in water tanks were dry; no sail, no mast, but two pieces of tarpaulin. I knelt down to search the after locker. Nothing odd there, but as I crawled backwards I saw a small bundle, wrapped in a sort of blue sailcloth and neatly stowed underneath the after thwart. I tucked the package into my shirt and, after a last check, I rejoined our cutter.

The sailors were absorbed in looking after the castaway and, when we were under the davits, we made a hash of hooking-on to the falls. I could feel the Old Man glaring down at me from the starboard wing. Precious minutes were being wasted, but finally we were slowly hoisted from the sea and *Eastern Princess* was underway again.

The doctor was waiting at the rail. He took charge and soon the wretched castaway was under surveillance in a sick bay bunk. I learned later that evening that it took the doc two hours to bring the poor devil round — and, even after that, it had been touch-and-go as to whether the survivor would live.

The incident had taken much longer than I had realized; when I regained the bridge to take over my watch again, I found that the second had already relieved me. The master was annoyed by the lost time and, just as I was about to report the details to him, Sparks arrived with the diversionary signal: we were ordered to alter for Charleston to pick up further cargo. I hung about for half an hour while the second and the master crouched over the charts, re-planning the passage. When finally I tried to get in a word, the Old Man snapped my head off and sent me packing. As far as he was concerned, the incident was over.

At dinner that night, the doc told us that the castaway would live, if he could survive the next twenty-four hours. He was presumably Central European. There was no way of identifying him because he wore nothing save the tattered rags in which we had found him.

I had the middle that night, so I turned in early, promising myself that I would look at the package during the quiet of the following day. So it was not until another twenty-four hours had passed that I had the chance to open the bundle. Although it was in my possession, no one else had seen it, however hard I tried to bring it to the notice of the master. Already I had begun to feel a sense of guilt.

I drew the curtain across the door of my cabin and settled down at my desk, just before the evening session in the saloon. I carefully unwrapped the sailcloth; inside was a sheaf of papers, at least three inches thick. Neatly strapped to the bundle with a half-perished rubber band was the stub of a soft pencil. I thumbed through the sheaf of closely-typed pages, which seemed to be in Russian characters. The pages were neatly numbered but the last few were in longhand and almost indecipherable; the writing scrawling across the crumpled sheets was faded with age or by sunlight. The handwriting finally petered out in anguished hieroglyphics. The dinner gong was sounding, so I carefully replaced the package in my locker and turned the key.

Shipboard life became very hectic the next day, because the mate went down with food poisoning. We were watch-on, watch-off for over a week, but eventually we reached Charleston, where the chief officer recovered sufficiently to resume duty. We handed over the castaway to the US authorities, who told us later that he was definitely insane and probably would never recover. The last we saw of the poor soul was when we watched him being hustled across the gangway to the ambulance and the psychiatric ward.

So it was not until we were well across the North Atlantic that I had another chance to inspect the pile of written pages. I had half-forgotten the matter and had ignored the promptings of my conscience, for, to be truthful, I was beginning to relish this strange incident which I had kept to myself. The mystery made a welcome break from the boredom of daily routine. I needed the advice of my elder brother. He was a junior professor at a university and had qualified in foreign languages, specializing in Russian. The result was that, just under a year later, the mad survivor's story was staring at me from a neatly typed and assembled manuscript which Geoff had translated into English.

The few pages which follow are the castaway's introduction to the strange tale he has to tell. They were probably added just before he finished the diary, which explains his weak handwriting. I think my brother has done well. He has translated the pages just as the writer recorded them.

Here it is, then, the anonymous castaway's introduction, unexpurgated and unaltered:

My name is Alexei Slepak. I am twenty-five and was born in a small town outside Tallin in what was once Estonia. If these pages of mine are ever found, I want the free world to know what I have written.

Because I also qualified (I came first in my class) in foreign political studies, I have thought much about how to present the characters in my diary: how to cast the actors in this tragedy, so that readers in the West can best identify themselves with these terrible events. We in Russia are different in so many ways and for so many different reasons, that it would be difficult for you in the West to understand us — and, in particular, the mind and workings of the Soviet Navy. My specialist thesis for my PhD (as you would term it) was *The Administration and Structure of the British Navy*. I have therefore thought it helpful to base this record upon the workings of a navy in the free world and, because of my research for my thesis, the obvious choice was the structure, ranks and ratings of the British Royal Navy, the service upon which the modern Soviet Navy was largely moulded.

The essential thing has been to tell the truth as I saw it, however painful. I am adding this 'introduction' because, if the authorities ever get hold of my record, the truth will be utterly distorted.

Above all else, I want Katya and her family to know that to the end I have tried not to fail them. God, I have tried — even to the final, horrible climax when I was forced to… [The handwriting then sloped off into an unintelligible scrawl which was beyond translation. There had evidently been a superhuman effort of will, for the writer's longhand gradually resumed a semblance of form again — his final words were on the next and last page of his Introduction — Derek Warne.]

It is not only the societies and empires of the West which are crumbling into the past, as man searches for a more equitable structure by which to order his affairs without sacrificing his freedom.

In my Mother Russia too, the voice and the aspirations of the little man are also gnawing, bit by bit, at the roots of the monolithic giant which decrees his destiny. The New Order which our parents and our grandparents accepted so joyfully, my generation and our children have difficulty in accepting. Freedom is like a seed: once it has germinated, it will push through the darkness until it reaches the light.

You, dearest Katya, will have received my last letter, so you will have realized that I can do no more. If this work ever sees the light of day, you will know that I had no choice. A man remains a man, only if he sustains his beliefs to the end: you taught me this, Katya, and this I have done. May our God go with you, Katya, my dearest Katenka.

CHAPTER ONE

She lay on the fresh spring turf, watching the galleon-clouds sweeping across the blue sky above her. Propped on one elbow, her physics book still unopened, she had looked forward to this lunchtime break in the open air with Alexei Slepak.

Maya Borisova was twenty-three. With only seven months to go before her finals, she could smell the sweet whiff of a good diploma, a vital step towards a responsible career. She glanced again towards the fountain where Alexei would have to pass.

She sighed, trying to ward off the demon of self-pity that too often swamped her. Had she made the greatest mistake of her life by choosing Leningrad for her training? She was a stranger among her roommates in the hostel, and the first year had been a hell of loneliness and self-doubt.

The comfortable two-roomed flat which her mother had made into a home was a far-off dream at the moment, and she yearned for distant Ulyanovsk, the town which had been home to her since childhood. Life had been so hard in Western Siberia that her father had broken from his family ties in Surgut. He had cleared off to the west where he found work in Leningrad. He had always hankered for the sea, so he had soon joined the navy, four months before the Nazis invaded in 1941.

Maya's mother often talked to her about the Great Patriotic War, but Maya was bored by it all. Her father had rarely spoken about his survival in the nine-hundred-day siege of Leningrad, but the experience had left its mark. He had been wounded in the hip and walked with a permanent limp, and his psychological scars had left a deeper impression. He had returned to his native Surgut where he had tried settling into civilian life. Marrying Maya's mother had given her father the stability he had needed; he eventually succeeded in persuading her to move to Ulyanovsk, where he became manager of a factory making spare parts for the big farm tractors. Above all else, he had provided a secure home during those hard post-war years when Stalin was putting the country back on its feet. Ulyanovsk, birthplace of Lenin, took its name from his political pseudonym, so was left comparatively in peace during the purges. Maya's father had died in 1961, but she could still remember his wrinkled face clearly enough.

Maya glanced at her watch: Alexei was late — or perhaps he had shied off, suspicious of her unusual friendliness. She had saved the cherries for his arrival, but she would soon have to start thinking about returning to the city. The buses ran every half hour, but the town of Pushkin was three quarters of an hour from the university. Alexei had suggested the rendezvous here: was it because he enjoyed the solitude in the parks surrounding the lycée, or because he did not want to be seen with her?

Slepak was a curious mixture. Realistic and ambitious, he nevertheless had a streak of mysticism about him which attracted her. She had been surprised when he had suggested coming all this way to Alexander Pushkin's town, where the poet had written his first verse.

It was strange how fate worked. They had studied in the same group for so long, yet neither had taken much notice of the other, each being too absorbed in work. It was only when they had, quite independently, both opted for the same specialization in sound and light, that they had begun seriously to discuss together the problems posed by these precise sciences.

Yesterday evening, they had shared the same table in the canteen. Alexei had paid for Maya's coffee and afterwards they had walked together. On their way to her hostel, she had confessed the boredom and loneliness she suffered in the six-bedded room which was now her home. He had understood — and that was the first moment that this drastic solution had stolen into her mind; but she would have to see what sort of a man he was first.

She felt a hand on her shoulder. She twisted round: Alexei Slepak, tall and deep-chested, was standing on the grass behind her. She scrambled to her feet and tucked the blouse into her skirt. She faced him while he regarded her, his pale blue eyes on a level with hers; he stood apart from her, a quirk of a smile twitching at the corners of his wide mouth.

Two days ago, even after months of close association in the lecture halls, Maya would have been incapable of describing Alexei Slepak, other than that he seemed a quiet, pleasant boy, intelligent and neat, the top of their group. Facing him now in the seclusion of this sunlit Pushkin Park, she could study him more carefully. Free of surveillance here, she regarded this quiet Estonian with fresh curiosity.

'I was worrying about my afternoon's lectures,' she said. 'I was thinking of leaving.'

Alexei Slepak looked older than his twenty-two years. He already bore crescent lines of cynicism at the corners of his mouth, but his rounded face was full of humour and a zest for life. He wore his fair hair too long for university conformity.

'Have we time to eat together?' he asked.

Maya pulled him down to the grass and held out the cherries. 'I'm well ahead with my work,' she said. 'The prof can do without me for one afternoon.'

Alexei had crossed the park from the other entrance and could see the fountain in the far distance. As he approached it, the sun's rays were trapped in a cloud of rainbow colours where the water showered upwards, before cascading into the bowl beneath.

Maya had been lolling on the grass, her back to him as she watched the people strolling in from the lycée: he would have recognized her tall figure anywhere. Aloof and uncommunicative, she had erected a barrier around herself which none of his contemporaries now bothered to surmount. She was an enigma, and men of his age could not be bothered with prickly women. Alexei had always been faintly amused by her: why did she have to wave her 'keep off' banner so energetically? She looked very capable of fending for herself.

He had halted to watch her unawares: she lounged on the warm grass, her long, sturdy legs stretching out from the navy blue skirt. As she lay there, propped on her elbows, her unusual height was not so noticeable. Perhaps she was over-sensitive about the daunting effect of her size; or perhaps, as a stranger from the east, she felt herself a rarity among her Leningrad roommates. Whatever the cause, Maya was a formidable woman.

Alexei had felt a sympathy for her and had been surprised at her eagerness to meet him here this afternoon. Observing her closely for the first time, he began to sense the woman in her: her long, thick-set neck, half-concealed by her disciplined, close-cropped brown hair; her high cheekbones accentuating her pallid skin; and her grey, wide-set eyes beneath her broad forehead. Reclining on her elbows, her heavy shoulders braced beneath the sleeveless white blouse which she was wearing for this hot June day.

Incongruous as it may have been, this woman and he were teetering on the edge of an affair which would certainly lead nowhere. He too needed companionship, as much as she apparently did. This university life admitted no privacy — they were all registered numbers, fed into the educational computer. When they were trained, they would each be appointed to jobs already planned for them. *No hit-and-miss about our Soviet system*, he thought. Unlike in the West, graduates from the universities were slotted directly into posts allocated to them by the State after graduation.

'You've only taken two,' Maya was saying. 'Don't you like them? I could demolish the lot.'

She was dangling a couple of the plumpest cherries above his lips as he lay stretched out beside her. The tips of her fingers were brushing his lips while she fed the fruit to him. Alexei opened his eyes, idly following the clouds sailing in the blue above them. He said nothing, and spat out the stones.

Maya stretched out beside him on the fresh, new grass. They remained silent, content in the present. In the background, the fountain splashed; Alexei heard the cries of the children and, distantly, the clamour of a passing train.

'Glad you weren't at the lecture this morning,' he said. 'You wouldn't have enjoyed it.'

'What happened? Old Frunze again, rambling on about the new formulae?'

'Wish it had been. We may have gone too far this time, Maya.' Alexei propped himself on one elbow, looking down at her.

The smile in her grey eyes vanished. 'The Party again?' she asked.

He nodded. Instinctively, he turned his head to be sure that they were still marooned on their green islet. 'Yuri didn't turn up this morning,' he said, lowering his voice.

'Celebrating last night? It was his birthday, wasn't it?'

Alexei shook his head. 'During the break, a list of seven names was put up on the board: five men, two women. They have to report to the office. But Yuri's wasn't on the list. I was suspicious, so I phoned through to his digs.'

'Vodka?'

He shook his head. 'His old crone of a landlady answered me. She wouldn't say much — just that a stranger had rung the bell and asked for Yuri. They went off together. On my way to the bus I looked in, but she was frightened. "An official," was all that I could get out of her.'

Maya was gathering her things together. 'You know Yuri well, don't you?' she asked.

'Yes — he's a good guy. And only last week…' Alexei was hesitating; he had to be sure of her before exchanging confidences. 'I've often wondered about Yuri,' he continued. 'He's a fanatic, an idealist prepared to risk his career for freedom's sake. Just over a month ago, he persuaded me to join his society. I signed up.'

'What society?' Maya was ready to leave. Her eyes were suspicious. Was he a fool to have said so much? But he was already committed.

'It's an organization to influence the Party: to halt the arrests, the persecution of our writers, scientists, mathematicians. It's a worldwide thing now, easy enough outside our homeland. Bloody dangerous here — I could be slung out from university tomorrow, if they get hold of the membership list. There's already a query against my name.'

'What've you done?'

'After being in the Young Pioneers, at fourteen I refused to try for Komsomol.'

'In Siberia, it's almost essential to be in the Young Communist League if you want a university place.'

'It's the same here, but they let me in: they told me afterwards that I came top of the results. They warned me to watch my step for the future.'

'And that's what worries you?'

Alexei rolled onto his side, the better to watch her. 'My name's on the noticeboard. I'll report this evening if you'll come with me.'

'I'm one of the two women?'

'Yes, Maya. Nina's the other.'

Maya sat up, staring at the fountain. Her full lips pouted. 'At least we share something — we've both got a prospective black mark against us.'

'We'll be stuck with that for a long time. And I meant to go far, Maya. I'm dead keen on my specialization. Light, sound and their allied sciences fascinate me. Look at where they've got us — to the planets and back.' He had only talked to Yuri like this. She must realize what a risk he was taking with her. But she might understand: Maya was very different from the others on campus.

Alexei was trying to mask his outburst by hauling her to her feet, but she was reluctant to move. A tussle on the grass of the lycée park was not the best way to remain inconspicuous. She stretched out fully, arched her back, then reached up for him.

Alexei held off, uncertain of himself. 'Come, Maya,' he said. 'We'd better be going. Let's get this visit over with. The office shuts at five.'

She was sulking when she sat up. There was reproach in her eyes as she hustled together the remains of their snack lunch.

'They may be turfing me out of my dormitory room,' he said. 'I'll have to find digs again. You know what that's like in Leningrad, in spite of the grant they give us.'

'They'll stop that too if you carry on in this way, Alexei,' Maya said crossly. 'Why've you always been a rebel? You show it even in lectures.'

Alexei remained silent, watching the trapped rainbow in the cascading fountain. 'Does it really show?'

Maya nodded, her hand carelessly brushing his. 'To me it does. You're a soft-hearted liberal, beneath that facade of yours. You don't like hurting people. You've got to be ruthless if you're to survive today. Look at our bureaucratic masters: all opportunists — and particularly at the top.'

'It's the same the world over. The more powerful the human specimen called a politician, the bigger the bastard.'

'These are the facts of life, Alexei: you can't change them. If you want to get anywhere, you've got to go along with them. Look where the dissidents end up — mental hospitals or exile.'

'I'll never quit our Russia.'

'That's what binds us together as a nation — nothing to do with the ideological manna with which they suckle us from birth.'

'We're a different breed from our parents. Stalin, Khrushchev and all the rest — even Brezhnev is in the historical dustbin. They're all irrelevant to our generation. Politics, even world politics, don't interest us anymore. I couldn't care less about uniting the workers of the world. Who wants to associate with some of those butchers?' He cursed in disgust. 'All I want is the chance to do my research: help the country, marry, raise a family eventually.' He realized with cold clarity that they were being swept along upon a torrent of intimacy — a dangerous exercise in these times, even in this post-Brezhnev era.

'And all I want,' Maya said as they strolled across the lawn, 'is to qualify and get back to my Ulyanovsk. It's a dull town, the country's flat, the winter's terrible — but it's lovely there. It's home.'

'Why d'you come here, then?' Alexei asked her quietly. 'I always wondered.'

'I had the choice of Rostov or Moscow. I hate most cities but I prefer the north, so I asked whether they'd take me at Leningrad. I thought a sea port would be tolerable.'

'And is it?'

'I detest my accommodation. They're bitches to me, even though I don't bother them.'

'How d'you mean?'

Maya was colouring, but the gatekeeper was watching them. 'I'll tell you next time,' she whispered. 'Here's the bus.'

She clutched his hand all the way as, in silence, they watched the countryside flashing past the window. They walked through the portals of the science faculty, then paused before entering the corridor to the students' office.

'Follow after me, Maya — twenty minutes' time. Offer them lip service — remember, if they sling us out, we'll never get a decent job.'

'You know why they've sent for me?' Maya asked softly.

'No idea.'

'I've a suspicion someone's found the book Nina lent me. I've kept it in my personal locker. While you're in the office, I'll nip up to the room to see if it's still there. I was going to return it to her tomorrow.'

'Porn?'

'Of course not,' Maya whispered. 'Worse than that.'

Alexei's eyebrows were arched in question.

'*Gulag*,' she said softly. '*The Archipelago*.' Then she departed, walking briskly towards the path which led to the women's hostel.

CHAPTER TWO

It was ten days later. Maya hesitated when she entered their communal bedroom after supper. She had waited for all her roommates, but Nina, the eldest and the only woman with whom Maya shared any sort of contact, was the last to arrive for bed.

'Is your Sergei coming tonight, Nina?' Maya asked abruptly.

'He's on night shifts this week.' The woman looked up, resentment in her brown eyes.

'You, Rai,' Maya asked the petite blonde in the corner bed. 'Is Boris coming?'

Rai lowered the journal she was reading. She looked up and stared. 'Nosey, aren't you, Maya Borisova? As it happens, he's not.'

'What about you, Tanya?'

But Tanya was already asleep, as were the other two. Maya turned to Nina, who was glancing sideways at her.

'What's bothering you, Maya?' Nina asked, smirking. 'You're all twitched up. You haven't got a man?'

'Tonight,' Maya said calmly. 'If none of you mind, Nina. His name's Alexei.'

'Why should I mind, dear? You haven't had your turn yet.'

'*What d'you know?* Wake up, girls!' Rai cried, flinging down her magazine. 'Borisova's on duty tonight.' She leaned across and jabbed her neighbour's shoulder. 'Tanya, wake up. Our Siberian's got a man tonight.' Rai was leering up at Maya. 'Need any help, dearie? I'll take over, if you...'

'Shut up, Rai,' Nina snapped. 'Leave her alone.' She touched Maya's sleeve. 'Course we don't mind. Be happy, that's all.' She climbed into bed and turned off the light.

Maya hesitated: there was no need, then, to go down to the phone to cancel Alexei. She changed into her blue nightie and slid into bed. She would try to stay awake until half past twelve and then she would slip down to let Alexei in through the office entrance. The guardian had promised her he would be doing his rounds at that hour, and again at five thirty. The old man had winked as she'd slipped a bottle of vodka beneath his desk. The encounter had not been as embarrassing as Maya had feared. This was how they were compelled to organize their lives.

She drifted into sleep and dozed intermittently until she heard the clock chiming midnight. She was immediately awake, waiting for the hands on her watch to crawl through the next twenty-five minutes. She slipped into her tracksuit, noiselessly opened the door and tiptoed down the corridor to the stairs.

Maya Borisova did not dread the coming of winter in Ulyanovsk. The first dusting of frost on the roads, the mantle of white in the fields exhilarated her with the memories of walks with her mother through the birch woods. But here in Leningrad, pent up now for over three months in this studio flat with Alexei, the long evenings and the nights were twitching at her nerves.

Autumn had clamped down early this year. She felt the biting edge of the wind cutting through the ill-fitting window frame. She hitched up the plum coloured coverlet, which Alexei had bought second-hand in the market, across the pane. Squeezing her way past her silent companion, she pulled the chintz curtain across the rail. Turning her back upon him, she undressed and slipped into bed.

Alexei Slepak remained slumped in the only chair, his textbook propped on his lap. His silence was the most difficult trial which Maya had to endure. They no longer walked back together from university: he would always manage to arrive home after she had completed the shopping. Though he would help prepare the meal, their conversation was false, monosyllabic.

Maya pulled the blanket to her chin, curled into a ball and waited for the bed to warm. She could hear his breathing on the other side of the curtain, his form outlined against the light above the table. She turned towards him and lay motionless, staring at the kitchen wall, while she recalled these three months since that decisive day when they had married.

Their relationship had slowly developed after their meeting in Pushkin Park. Two days before the summer break, Alexei had received from the preceptor a notice to quit his dormitory — no reasons given. He may have been secretly sharing the same idea that had matured slowly in Maya's mind, but he gave no sign, even when she had dropped the hint. It had been after the summer break, with winter approaching, that she had invited him to her bed in the hostel.

Maya closed her eyes, trying to shut out the humiliation of that night. She could still hear the sniggers of Rai and the others, as Alexei had slipped from his clothes in the darkness. They had waited, rigid in each other's arms, for their invisible supervisors to drop off to sleep. Alexei had been unable to contain his impatience — and for her, as his hands sought to arouse her, silently caressing, the night had been painful and distressing. The effect of their silent companions, invisible in the half-darkness, inhibited him and their efforts were profoundly unsatisfactory for both of them.

He had stayed until the early hours but she had held him off, longing for sleep, disgusted by the whole messy business as he had tried again to satisfy her. Mercifully, the others had dropped off when she had finally pushed him out and taken him down at the appropriate hour of five.

She had been astonished when, in the lecture room the next morning, he had nonchalantly laughed off the disappointing night. It was his uninhibited understanding that had led her to suggest the solution to their mutual accommodation problems.

She had proposed marriage. As man and wife they would have priority on the housing lists and, if they were lucky, they would be sure of a roof over their heads until they finished their training.

She was convinced now that it had been the Yuri affair which had influenced him most: his motivation was not love, nor even lust, because she had frankly stated her terms. Unless they grew to love each other, they would divorce as soon as they had been appointed to their first jobs after gaining their degrees. The formula was common enough among their generation, whose accommodation difficulties in the cities were practically insoluble.

To her surprise, he had agreed at once to her proposed terms: they would not sleep together. No sex, no children. She would do the cooking, he would look after the house.

Normally, three months' notice was required by the authorities before the formalities of marriage could be arranged but, at this time of the year, the applications were less; they had managed to organize their ceremony for the middle of the autumn term.

Maya wore her green dress and Nina, her witness, was in a beige outfit. Alexei was in his light blue suit, but Maya had never before met his friend who acted as his witness.

When they arrived at the registry office at four o'clock (they were booked for four-thirty) they discovered that they were thirty-second in the queue — things were running late. It was half past six before they finally stood together in front of the director, a formidable dame. Her bosom was enveloped by a crimson sash upon which was emblazoned the emblem of the hammer and sickle and the injunction: *Workers of the World Unite*. The room was bare except for a desk and a pot of golden chrysanthemums in the corner. After the ceremony, the volume of the tape-recorder playing Tchaikovsky's *Sleeping Beauty* was turned up. The assistant coyly bade them embrace and then they were ushered from the room as the next couple elbowed past them.

They had shared a meal with their two witnesses, then had walked alone across the city, back to their hostels, where they'd immediately completed their application forms for the housing list. On Monday Alexei had taken the forms, backed by their marriage certificate, directly to the city housing offices.

During the waiting period they worked all hours, for this was their last term before finals, and they collected together what they could for the day when their luck would turn. Life had gone on as before, but with no repetition of the night they had spent together in the hostel. Then one morning Alexei had confronted her, a form fluttering in his hand. Three weeks later they were installed in Flat 13H of Tolstoi Tower, the newest block that the city authorities had built.

Maya was finding sleep impossible tonight. The memory of their first evening in this flat was still bitter. Alexei had tried to break her down but she had been adamant, reminding him of their contract: they were sharing the flat to work for their degrees and to win a good job, the one ambition in life which was important to her. They would share the flat, but not the bed. And, in spite of several roundabout attempts, he had kept his distance — until tonight, when he had become impossible. Why *was* he insisting that they should both go to the pop session? It was the last thing she wanted now.

Maya had thought that he was accepting this workmanlike solution to their accommodation problem. After the shock of rejection had passed, he had slipped into a sullen silence and she had trained herself to be careful about what she said. Then, two months ago, their relative tranquillity had been disturbed by his sudden, extraordinary outburst. What a strange man Alexei was: she watched him behind the curtain, a motionless silhouette crouched over his book. She was beginning to understand the workings of a man: his moroseness was caused by a range of factors. She remembered the words of her mother with whom she had lived for so long: 'All men are the same. They take everything.' Maya had not detected what lay behind the outburst, but she could understand now. Until that night two months ago, she had tried to give Alexei the companionship they both craved.

That night he had arrived home earlier than usual. His sullenness had been particularly icy. As she was undressing, he had whipped back the curtain. She had just dropped her bra on the bed. Confronting her, he had devoured her nakedness. He had blurted angrily: 'Don't you know what it's like? Isn't it the same for a woman?'

Maya had stood quite still, allowing his eyes to roam over her. For the first time, she felt the thrill of anticipation: a man wanted her. She had remained there, motionless, waiting for his anger to abate. Then she had held her hands out to him. Alexei had stepped forwards to take her into his arms.

'But we don't love each other,' she whispered.

'It's time you grew up, Maya. That may come later.'

She had given in, but it had been for the last time. He had made love to her the whole night through, but it had been merely a more prolonged repetition of their night in the hostel. His ineptitude had driven him to a series of spasmodic attempts, but the more frenzied he became the more she was repelled by his performance. She had been thankful when at last, her back to his, she had glimpsed the first light of dawn stealing through the chinks in the ill-fitting coverlet across the window. She had lain rigid so as not to arouse him until, at the last moment, she had woken him for his morning lectures. He had sensed her repulsion, and from that day onwards he had lapsed into this sullen remoteness. He had never bothered her again until yesterday evening, when she had broken the news to him: the pregnancy tests were positive. Even flippancy would have been better than his silence.

He was scraping back the chair, preparing his camp bed for the night. Maya turned her back on him, burying her face in the pillows, as another wave of nausea swept through her.

CHAPTER THREE

The springs creaked behind the curtain. Maya must be turning in the bed, presumably with her back to him. Maya Slepak, his legal wife… Alexei Slepak groaned as the future stretched aridly before him.

'Why won't you come out tonight?' he repeated for the third time. 'The Combos are only in Leningrad for two days, before they go back to Moscow. It's only half past eight now.'

The curtain-rings screeched as she whipped aside the chintz. She was sitting up, half-turned to him in her buttoned-up nightdress. Her grey eyes were smouldering with resentment.

'It's your fault I'm like this,' she snapped. 'I'm tired. Can't you understand? Go on your own. I'm not stopping you.'

'It'll do you good,' he insisted, 'to get out for a bit.' He slid the chair towards her and took her hand. 'Come on, Maya — what are you afraid of?'

She pushed him away. 'I don't understand you, Alexei. You're in enough trouble already, without going to the pop session. You know that Valentin Chakovsky is in trouble with the police. And just before the finals … with me like this…'

Alexei stood up, pulled on his anorak and walked out, slamming the door behind him.

Valentin Chakovsky's group, The Combos, had clandestinely acquired a derelict, ex-factory canteen on the seedier side of the industrial estate, five kilometres from the city centre. Alexei Slepak took the bus across the Neva, then jumped off at the Bolshoy Bridge. He walked across it, the city lights reflecting below him in the black waters of the Malaja. As he left the trees of the park to his right, the fortress of St Peter and St

Paul reared gaunt and black in the night. Now a museum, its buildings were still a sinister reminder of the days when it had housed its many prisoners.

Alexei crossed the broad boulevard and strode out towards the suburbs. This was the second night of The Combos' performance. Another couple in the physics class had lost their nerve at the last moment and had refused to pay the black market price for the tickets. Alexei had eagerly accepted them, so here he was, the Malaja gliding silently past him on his left, and a wasted ticket in his pocket. He could still feel the resentment within him, angry with himself as much as with his 'wife' whom he had left sulking in her bed.

So Maya was pregnant. If she now changed her mind and refused divorce after they had gained their diplomas, he was stuck with her — responsible for her and the child that neither of them wanted, forced to live with her in misery that would turn swiftly to hate. What a horrible mess he had landed them both in — to live with her cold, calculating brain, sharing the same room, without even sex as a sedative, for as long as he could see into the future.

A cat streaked across the deserted street. Two policemen, their breath steaming in the bitter cold as they strolled down the opposite pavement, stared at him as he hurried past. A woman, exercising her dog, swore at him beneath her breath as he inadvertently tripped over the animal's lead.

Number 147 Dolinsk Road — a derelict old factory canteen, Yuri had said. He passed two more turnings, then saw in the distance the roofs of the factory buildings, gaunt against the indigo, star-studded night. He traversed an open square, leaving a group of dark-coated men circling each other cautiously in the shadows — probably a huddle of *fartsovshchiki*, a ring of black marketeers swapping the latest pop records smuggled in from the West.

Alexei Slepak turned down the earmuffs of his fur hat and thrust his hands deep into the pockets of his anorak. Keeping parallel to the Malaja Neva, he followed the tributary until he reached the seedy outskirts of the industrial estate: squat ventilation towers; wire fences; potholes gouged out of the road by heavy transport; crumpled *Pravda* pages fluttering across the road... There it was, leading off to the right, Dolinsk Road, narrow and flanked by a succession of one-storied, light industrial buildings. There was no street lighting here; the road was dark where it narrowed towards the cul-de-sac in the distance. He strode onwards and then, when he thought he had passed it, he heard the pop music thumping from a peeling derelict building. He was about to try the door when a man loomed from the darkness.

'The Combos?' Alexei asked.

'Got a ticket? Come inside.'

The sound hit them when the door opened. They slipped inside and the large official held out his hand for the precious passport to this clandestine gathering. Alexei pulled out the tickets.

'What d'you have two tickets for?' The man was suspicious. 'Selfish bugger, aren't you? There's a couple here we're turning away because they've only got one.' He beckoned across the packed hall to another official, who began threading his way through the mob.

'Hey, Ivan — this guy's got two tickets.'

The older man glanced at Alexei. 'How d'you get them?'

'Through the normal channels. My wife couldn't come.' They were shouting above the amplifiers when a couple approached from the rear.

'This woman hasn't got a ticket. Will you let her have yours?'

Alexei handed the scrap of grey paper across to the young woman. The man with her began rummaging in his pocket.

'That's okay,' Alexei said. 'It would have been thrown away.' The officials disappeared into the crowd.

'Thanks,' the stranger shouted. 'We were just leaving; we could only raise one ticket.' He glanced at his companion, a small, darkhaired woman with serious brown eyes. 'Katya Lazareva — and I'm Lev Barabanov. I'm on two days' leave from the navy and I haven't seen Katya since we were kids. We're cousins.'

They shook hands, then turned to watch the group on the stage, bashing out the beat. 'Stick around,' Barabanov yelled in Alexei's ear. 'We'll share a jar afterwards.'

There was no seating and the hall was crammed. Alexei stood behind Barabanov and the woman; they were immediately sucked into the enthusiasm of the audience, every one of whom, Alexei realized, was risking trouble with the authorities. Though this clandestine challenge to authority provided the spice for these gatherings, it was the music which brought them here on this freezing night.

'Watch Valentin Chakovsky,' Lev shouted in Alexei's ear. 'Great, isn't he?'

The Combos' leader was swaying to the liquid notes spilling like crystal drops from his clarinet. His eyes were closed, his body arched like a bow bent backwards as his fingers coaxed the magical notes. To his left, a youth was crouched over his electric guitar, plucking the throbbing rhythm from the strings. The drummer, a bearded man in his late twenties with Beatle-type spectacles, his eyes glazed, his mouth hanging open, was thrashing hell out of the cymbals until the sound crashed around the hall. A cheer rang to the ceiling as the tempo suddenly changed.

'Valentin's got guts, Lev,' the woman was shouting. 'How's he survived?'

'He's intelligent.'

Alexei remembered the idol's reputation: Chakovsky, in the daytime a hard-working teacher, had developed his 'jazz' group for the benefit of the authorities who discouraged contemporary pop. He gave his official performances at the Ministry of Culture's and Komsomol's concerts. The fifties dance tunes were an excellent cover for the pop which he had developed secretly with his group. The starved youth, hungry for modern music, had adopted him as one of their idols: he was now giving over thirty undercover sessions a year.

The music was throbbing to the rafters, the amplifiers at full volume. Alexei felt the thrill of being part of this dedicated tribe. Pop was their common language, something only their generation could understand. They were all real people here, not puppets jigging to their masters' bidding. The difficulty was finding a ticket, which could only be wangled through persuasion or knowing the right contact. The news that a group would be coming to the city could only be known by keeping an ear to the ground.

It had been Yuri who had put Alexei on to this facet of life. The black market in pop records had reached a new peak this year, they said. To the authorities, this underground trade was worse than the West's drug problem — and censored groups like The Combos were the most dangerous elements, as far as the Party was concerned.

The group was flinging out its last number when Lev Barabanov nudged his elbow. 'We'll take Katya home and then we can have a drink.' They walked back to the Bolshoy Bridge and caught a bus to the Nevsky. They delivered Katya Lazareva to her parents, who were living in a two-roomed flat on the eleventh floor of a block off Lomonosov Street.

'Come and meet Nikolai and Lyudmila,' Lev said. 'He's in the navy too. They haven't been married long, but when I'm in Leningrad I stay with them.'

It was useless protesting. It was midnight when finally they were welcomed into the apartment only two blocks away. Nikolai, a short, stumpy man, produced the vodka and after ten minutes Lyudmila excused herself. 'I know you boys won't want me for a bit,' she said, taking her husband's hand. Their eyes met and Alexei felt a tinge of envy as the unspoken message flickered between them.

'We won't be long,' Lev said. 'I want Nikolai to meet Alexei — and I owe him a drink.'

Alexei settled himself into one of the three chairs, while Nikolai poured out the vodka. 'Steady,' Alexei protested. 'I'm not used to your navy tots.'

The alcohol went down in one. He waited for the spirit to fire his guts, then relaxed with the warmth.

'You met at The Combos? Any good?' Nikolai asked, refilling their glasses.

The conversation soon quit the banalities: these two were wholly absorbed by their profession. They slipped quickly into shop, but Alexei was content to remain only a bystander.

'Nikolai is in submarines,' Lev explained. 'I'm "up top" — in destroyers. We don't often meet.'

'How long have you been in the navy?' Alexei asked. 'Since university?'

Nikolai nodded. 'I'm only a "pressed" man, but I've signed on for a short service commission.' He grinned. 'Lev's a professional — in for life.'

'We have to tolerate you amateurs. But you don't dislike the life all that much, do you, Nikolai?'

'I was keen at first, but my enthusiasm's wearing a bit thin. The long nuclear patrols are boring. The bloody-mindedness of the troops gets on my nerves. I'll be glad to get back to conventionals.'

'Why don't you go for the hunter-killers? They're more interesting, surely?'

And so the shop went on: Nikolai, the enquiring, searching mind; Lev, the trained professional, dedicated to the service which, in less than ten years, had become the world's second most powerful naval force.

'We owe it all to Gorshkov,' Lev said. 'I met him once. He inspected us in the training ship.'

'Were you *Volga*?'

'No, *Tobol*.'

'That's why we've never met, then.'

Lev nodded. 'I'm doing the Staff College next September.'

'Lenin Academy, here?'

Lev nodded. In the short silence, Nikolai again recharged their glasses. 'Pity we short service lot can't be selected for the Academy,' he said, holding out the bottle. 'It would help morale.'

'Can't all be brilliant,' Lev said. He turned to Alexei, a sardonic smile creasing his clean-cut face. 'Why don't you consider the navy? We need scientists, particularly your variety.'

A happy haze had begun to envelop Alexei. To hell with his problems with Maya — that could wait until the morning. Through the tobacco smoke he watched the two officers, type-cast in the service which was forcing the world to heed the Soviet Union's demands. They were so obviously proud of what they represented, of what they were doing. What must life be like, committed to narrow lines, knowing exactly where you were going?

'Tell me, Lev,' Alexei challenged. 'Why should I join your set-up? What's so great about it?'

The others laughed. Nikolai began singing 'The Red Flag'.

'Shut up,' Lev said, grinning. 'You're pissed.' He got up and slapped Nikolai on the back. 'Listen, I'll tell you just why. For one thing, we need idiots like you. Give him another tot, Kolya. We'll have him signing on, if he doesn't watch it.'

Alexei allowed them to have their say. They were schoolboys in their enthusiasm. They, like him, were feeling the vodka. It was difficult to focus as they droned on about the joys of being a sailor. Poor sods, couldn't they see past their noses? And yet, was there some sense in what they were proclaiming, especially in these unstable days?

Nikolai had risen from his chair again, when his wife drifted quietly into the room. 'You'll be waking the neighbours,' she said. 'It's nearly two, Kolya.'

'Come along, Alyosha,' Lev said, struggling to his feet. 'I'll see you home. I can finish my recruiting spiel on the way.'

Alexei tottered to his feet, the walls swirling around the grinning face of his host. 'G'night, Kolya... G'night, Lyudmila Ivanovna.'

'Get going, Alyosha. You're drunk.' Lev was gripping his arm and shoving him through the door. 'Go to bed,' Lev called back over his shoulder. 'You lucky people. I'll see our civilian home.'

The freezing air hit them as they set their course for the Nevsky and on towards the flat. Alexei did his best to follow, but his feet would not coordinate. He stopped to puke into the gutter. Lev took his arm again and together they staggered across the city to the Suvorovsky Boulevard. Lev did not stop talking, but Alexei caught little of what he was saying — the conversation was moons away.

'Thanks, Lev,' Alexei mumbled. 'This is my pad. I'm home now. Nice evening.'

'I'll see you up to your flat.'

'Okay now. G'night.'

Alexei grasped his grinning companion by the shoulders and turned him about. Lev disappeared in the direction from which they had come, and Alexei was glad to be on his own again. He had sobered up and the street lighting was pirouetting less crazily. There was the tobacconist's shop. This was the block, this the prison where he lived. He found the entrance, pressed the button and stumbled into the lift.

He fell over the chair in the darkness. The bedside light snapped on.

'You're drunk,' Maya said. 'It's past three.' She was sitting bolt upright, blinking owlishly in the light, her face creased with pink blotches. 'What sort of trouble have you got yourself into now?'

'Made some new friends,' Alexei said. 'Nice people.' He felt a fool standing there, a stranger in his own home. The memory of Nikolai and his Lyudmila swum before him, for their silent intimacy and unspoken love. He flung his anorak across the fallen chair.

'Get to bed,' Maya snapped. 'And don't pull the plug — you'll wake the whole floor.'

CHAPTER FOUR

Maya woke at five. Her mind churned around their hopeless future; how was she to continue living with this man with whom she had nothing in common? The alarm buzzed at six-thirty, and she edged from her bed. Stepping over Alexei's snoring body, she slipped into her housecoat and tiptoed to the minute bathroom. She closed the door behind her and turned on the light.

The face looking back at her from the mirror was drawn, the cheeks grey and pasty. She combed savagely at her close-cropped hair. Her eyes were staring back at her in discontent — and beneath this beige gown a new life would soon be stirring.

Maya resented this cruel stroke of fate: she did not want the kid and nor did he. If she did not have to wait for her exam results, she would immediately pack up her things and go straight back to Ulyanovsk. Alexei Slepak was no good to her. Still resentful, she completed her toilet and returned to the living-room, where she snapped on the light. She stood over the recumbent body on the camp bed, contempt sweeping through her. She prodded the foot of his bed with her toe.

His mouth hung open and he was snoring loudly. His chin was grey with stubble and there was a slither of slime at the corner of his mouth. She leaned down and shook his shoulder.

'Aren't you going to lectures this morning?'

He blinked when the light hit him, groaned, and pressed his head between his hands. 'Uh! God, my head…'

'Lectures this morning — aren't you going?'

He propped himself on one elbow and shook his head gingerly.

'Sorry, I forgot,' Maya said. 'Habit, I suppose.'

'My results are out today. No lectures. Ten days before yours are announced, isn't it?'

Alexei was staring up at her, sobered by the dawning of reality. They looked at each other, but he did not speak: in that instant, loathing and despair were showing in his pale-blue eyes. She knew, then, that the end had come. She could never love this man, let alone respect him. She could never forget last night — and by his eyes, neither would he. When he had sobered up in the early hours, he had tried to approach her; but the alcoholic fumes and the memory of her drunken father had been too much for her.

'About ten days,' Maya said. 'That's all they would tell us.'

Alexei remained on the camp bed, staring sullenly up at her. 'What are you going to do?'

Maya evaded the question. 'I'm off to do the shopping. Nina said a consignment of shoes was expected in the store today.' She pulled the curtain across and began dressing. 'I've put on the tea. You can get your own breakfast.' As she said it, she wished she had been more gentle with him. She reached for her coat, studiously avoiding him, then shut the door of the flat behind her.

She was thankful to reach the crisp morning air and to mingle with the crowds spilling from their homes to work. The People's Store would not be crowded at this hour, she hoped.

She pushed against the swing door of the department store and made her way to the third floor, the shoe department. So often she was either too early or too late to catch the elusive imports from Czechoslovakia or Poland. A queue had already formed at the counter, a line straggling half the length of the floor.

'How long has the queue been here?' Maya asked the woman in front of her. 'I'm all right for the new shoes, aren't I?'

'Since the doors opened.' She nodded and smiled kindly.

A woman stumbled into her from behind; she put down her basket. 'Shoes?' she asked. 'I've been in the wrong queue. They've got a lot of gloves in from Poland on the first floor.'

The old woman's face was loaded with cunning: Maya was an old hand at this game, and Nina was generally right; her boyfriend worked in the docks and knew what was what. 'Here I am,' Maya muttered to herself, 'and here I stay.' She splayed her sturdy legs and prepared for a long siege — until the lunch hour if need be, which was not so unusual a wait for shoes.

She was finding that she was tiring more easily now. The doctor at the university clinic (too old and she didn't like his familiar approach) had confirmed what she had already calculated — but how were Alexei and she to see the time out? Life was unpleasant enough now — but, as she became more embittered, how would he react? One thing was certain: as she became larger and uglier, he would surely lose his randiness. That would be a relief, for she couldn't bear his touch now — and then there was last night. By the sullen, silent accusation in his eyes this morning, he seemed to be loathing himself and the sight of her. *Hard luck*, she thought.

But the child — what to do about it? Alexei would stick to their contract, she was sure of that. In a few days' time, she would be free to pack up. Would it be better for them to stick together?

The thought of this continuing agony beneath the same roof had already demolished any softer feelings she might have had for him. Her vacillation was one of the extraordinary things about her pregnancy: one minute her morale was high, the next, rock-bottom.

And Alexei, too — he was impossibly scratchy now. He had been working such long hours that she was convinced he was unbalanced: he would latch on to some trivial complaint and make mountains out of it. Everything was becoming out of proportion for them both.

It was as well that they could now see each other as they really were, without falsity. This morning Alexei Slepak, her legal husband, had showed up in his true colours. He was a selfish brute. Life with him, even if they stayed together because of the coming child, was bound to be hell. Better to part now, without too much bitterness. The health people would be bound to approve an abortion, if she had no means of support because of the disappearance of her husband and an impending divorce. She continued to think along these lines as the queue crawled forwards.

Maya felt the tension building inside her. It would take little to burst into a flood of tears; people became different animals in these queues. Last week she had waited an hour and a half to buy an enamel saucepan from Poland. When she reached the head of the queue, the counters had been switched and so she was in the queue for Czech coffee-grinders — the saucepans had been shifted to another counter on the floor above. She bought the grinder, even though she did not need it. One might never find the opportunity again.

The man five places ahead of her was shouting at the clerk. The sales woman was shrugging her shoulders and setting up a plaque in front of her: *Sold out.* The man was red with fury and shaking his fists at her. The woman had rung her electric bell. From the far corner of the store, Maya watched a green-coated official bearing towards them. She extricated herself from the disappointed trail of humanity and slowly walked away.

Suddenly, everything was too much for her. A dam broke and tears began streaming down her face. People pushed past unheeding, scurrying towards the lifts. She would have to hurry to the food department, if she was to get a meal before she left again for her afternoon final exam. There was bound to be another queue after the pay point at the check-out point, where some of the shoppers were put through the procedure of having their bags inspected. Shoplifting had to be prevented somehow, she supposed.

It was twenty-five minutes past one when Maya finally rang the bell of their flat. Alexei opened the door and helped her, in silence, to unload and pack away the food. She had made up her mind to break the news of her decision at once. She took off her coat, hung it on the hook behind the door and turned towards him. He was standing by the table, his hands behind his back. He seemed pale, and there was a tension about him she had not seen before.

'Sit down, Maya. You won't like what I've got to say.'

She lowered herself into the chair and faced him. He was silhouetted against the window and she could not see his eyes properly.

'Well, what is it? Did you get your degree?' Her heart was hammering in the silence of the room. 'I want to talk too.'

'I'm joining the navy,' he announced shortly. 'I signed on this morning. They're short of communication specialists and my degree suits them. They'll have me in a fortnight's time, if I pass the interview.'

CHAPTER FIVE

The only reasonable train to Ulyanovsk via Moscow was the 23:43 night express. Therefore, Maya and Alexei had spent their last day together, Friday, 21 February, in a state of strain and apprehension at the final parting. Neither spoke of the future. The day dragged interminably, but at last they were here on Platform 14, a trolley loaded with Maya's gear.

The other five occupants of her compartment were already ensconced. In silence, Alexei tucked her baggage away and coped with the trunk. It was just eleven-thirty, so they descended again to the platform.

'Will you write?' he asked.

'D'you want me to?'

'Yes. About the baby…'

'There won't be a baby.' She looked away, stared towards the ticket barrier and folded her arms. 'I'm going to make a fresh start.' She turned to him, adding, 'Try to forget.'

'The quicker the better, for both of us. It was my fault. I'll do all I can about the divorce.'

'Thanks. Good luck with the sale of the furniture.'

'I'll send you your half of the cash. I hope the flat lets easily.'

'You've got to give a month's notice. Don't forget.'

'Tomorrow.'

Maya brushed his forehead with her lips. 'I'd better get in.'

'Okay.' Alexei helped her up the step. She wound down the window opposite her compartment; she was trying to smile, but her eyes were hard. He glanced at the vast clock — two minutes to go.

The controller further up the platform was glancing at his watch. His baton was already in his hand.

'Goodbye, Alexei.'

A whistle shrilled. The train jerked; a diesel engine roared from somewhere ahead. Alexei looked up at her; he choked with emotion, unable to speak.

He stood motionless on the platform until the two red lights on the rear coach disappeared into the complex of the distant signal system. Then he walked slowly back along the platform, one regret churning through his mind.

''Ere, comrade,' the ticket collector at the barrier was saying. 'Where's your platform ticket?'

Alexei scrabbled in the pocket of his anorak and finally produced the scrap of paper.

'All right, are yer?'

He walked on. He had not even called 'goodbye' to her.

From the moment of their decision to part, Alexei Slepak had made a pact with himself that he would not allow morbid self-pity or remorse to wreck the next few days. The vodka bottle had helped, when he had finally stumbled into bed on that Friday night, but he had worked over the weekend, regularizing his papers and planning for the future. On Monday he was to collect his diploma at the presentation ceremony, a good honours degree, in spite of his recent difficulties. Maya had arranged with the university for her certificates to be forwarded to her at Ulyanovsk. She, too, had done well, which was consoling: she could look forward to a decent job. And he had, last week, successfully passed his medical and interview: he was to officially join the navy next Sunday, 1 March.

He did not hear from Maya, neither did he expect to. He thrust the past behind him and used the week to tie up the loose ends. On the Monday afternoon, he went to the housing office and handed in his notice to quit. If a tenant could be found (even the city rents were beyond most students now), he could stop paying the rent as from the first of April. He typed out an inventory of the bits of furniture he had to sell and distributed the notices throughout the district during Tuesday.

He had evaded the ordeal of confronting his parents. But, with the flat so depressingly condemning, he decided to go down to Tallin on the Wednesday to see them. His father had at first been scornful, but his mother's conciliation had eased the tension. Alexei had cut himself off from them since his marriage, and this insensitivity had pained them most. His visit had reassured them; when he had left them on this Saturday to return to his flat for the night, the close relationship which they had previously enjoyed had been re-established. While packing his cases this evening, he realized that this was his last day as a civilian. This last night in the flat was one he would remember for a long while: the ghosts were too real.

The alarm pealed at six. Sunday, 1 March, and the snowflakes were fluttering down, white confetti against the street lighting outside. He shaved while the water heated for tea. 'Report at the barracks at 0900,' they had told him, and he was glad he had ordered the taxi. At a quarter past eight, he turned the key in the lock of his door. Life would never be the same again. He sat back in the cab, watching the meter ticking up its charge.

'Where to?'

'Naval Barracks — the wardroom.' He felt self-conscious, not yet used to the idea that soon he would be a member of an elite class, an officer in the Soviet Navy. He settled back and watched the snowflakes drifting across the window.

They had only recently introduced this new scheme for graduate entry; he was one of the first to be so admitted. With a good degree behind him, he would be specializing in communications as soon as he finished his basic training, which was to take two years ashore instead of the usual five. At the beginning of his third year, he would be going to sea in his specialization, instead of spending a further three years ashore on specialist training. Sergei Gorshkov, their remarkable Admiral of the Fleet and 'Boss' of the navy, had worked miracles by building up the Soviet Navy in so short a time. He knew what he wanted and had won his battles with the Central Committee CPSU. Though the lower deck was a conscript navy (three years for those at sea, two for the ratings ashore) the majority of the officer structure was volunteer.

'Here we are. Good luck.'

Alexei paid the driver outside the wardroom entrance. As he began struggling with his luggage, a sailor came running towards him; he saluted and picked up the heaviest of the bags.

'Follow me, sir. I'll take you to the hall porter.'

A bugle was sounding across the road. Through a wire fence, Alexei watched a swarm of seamen streaking across the vast parade ground. Except for the clatter of their boots, there was complete silence. A white flagstaff was in the centre, the red flag of the Soviet Union at its truck; the naval ensign (the red star, and hammer and sickle on their white ground, the blue band at the bottom) was fluttering from the gaff. Alexei Slepak felt a tinge of pride as he turned towards the wardroom entrance. A uniformed sentry, with fixed bayonet, was marching stolidly to and fro outside the doorway.

The next few weeks were for Alexei a mixture of frustration and amusement. A student and a relatively free agent for so long, as an acting sub-lieutenant (*mladshiy leytenant*) in the Soviet Navy, he found it difficult at first to accept without resentment that he could not come and go as he pleased. He was allowed one weekend's leave a month: fortunately, this was coinciding with the two days in which he had arranged to settle up the flat on Saturday, 28 March. He would stay the night and return to barracks on the Sunday night, after turning over the keys and selling the furniture to the new tenant.

The month had begun with another medical. After the thorough examination he had undergone before the interview, the barracks' affair had been a mere formality. The doc had felt his forehead, winced and declared, 'You're warm. You're in.' He had passed the vigorous eye test, so was eligible to become a watchkeeper and for eventual command.

The course had begun with the fundamentals common to all navies. 'Good for discipline!' the petty officer had boomed at his class of twenty-eight assembled for the first time on the parade ground, and for the remainder of the mornings during that first week they had been drilled in marching, countermarching and on how to give orders. At first Alexei had felt self-conscious playing at sailors. He had joined as a man, not as a youth, so the ritual grated more with him than with most of the others who were younger.

The small arms training on the ranges took place in the bitter winds during the afternoons while the light remained. After supper, though they craved sleep, the men were fed lectures on the structure and organization of the service. Admiral of the Fleet Sergei Georgiyevich Gorshkov was in a hurry and they all sensed this urgency, this pressure to overtake, both in numbers and in weaponry, the United States Navy, the only force which could, on its own, challenge the Soviet bid for world domination at sea.

One lecture per night was conducted by a political officer, a specialist in the branch of the political directorate. These commissars, who were now eligible to qualify for sea command, were carried in every ship. Their chief was responsible to the commander-in-chief of the navy, but he also had direct access to the main political directorate and so to the Party's central committee. The responsibility of the directorate was to indoctrinate the navy with the Party dogma; through its chain of command, it could bypass even the navy's Big Boss. It was not surprising that, even at Alexei's level, it was common knowledge that this fist in the velvet glove did not always produce harmonious relations at sea.

The political officer's influence was all-pervasive. During the course's first political lecture, the instructor had checked the register and read the nominal list in two sections: the first list bore the names of those who were Party members; the second, in which Slepak featured, contained those who had not yet earned a place in the Party. The lecturer had intimated that if his listeners wished to reach command and the higher echelons of the navy, they should be Party members. 'You can always come along and see me if you have any difficulties,' he ended paternally. 'We're responsible for welfare as well as for political training.'

The pressure had merely strengthened Alexei's distaste for coercion, but from that moment he had begun to consider cynically whether to try to become a member of the Party, if only for ease of promotion. Damn it, he could pay lip-service for self-interest, like so many of them. Yet for all that month, the rebel within him held him back. Why should he sell his soul, if he didn't believe in the credo? Their C-in-C, Gorshkov, had fostered in his officers an overriding ambition to get to sea. Being a Party member was not, they now said, an essential qualification for executive and final sea command — but it helped.

Alexei soon found that he and two other non-Party members tended to stick together: they would drink together in the canteen, join the same sporting options. By the end of the third week they were beginning to share confidences, though they were all instinctively cautious — one's future career was at stake.

By the end of the month, Alexei no longer felt awkward in his uniform, nor at the ritualistic saluting between officer and man. If an officer failed to return a rating's salute, he would be hauled up before the commissar within the hour. 'It's a matter of mutual respect,' they had been told. 'Don't ever forget that. Discipline, discipline, discipline.' With the lower deck almost entirely conscript, and with an entry of 60,000 raw recruits every six months, the efficient running of the navy depended on a rigid command structure. The sea-going sailor often spent his three years in the same ship, and when abroad was rarely allowed shore leave. Absolute obedience to his officers' orders was paramount, as everyone understood.

As the Saturday of his weekend approached, Alexei began to question whether he could follow this simple naval creed for long, and in the hours before dawn, when he would lie awake analyzing the mess he had so far made of his life, the demon of depression would smother him. Friday night finally arrived: he packed up his weekend grip and turned in early. At least the worry of the apartment would be off his mind by this time on Sunday.

Alexei stood in the entrance to the flat and closed the door slowly behind him. He had expected it to look different: tomorrow, at six in the evening, he would have handed over the key and, with luck, have sold the furniture to the new tenant.

There was the rumpled chair in which he had spent so many of his evenings during those months ... and the chintz curtain drawn back on its rail. He tried to shake the despair from his soul as he started to unpack his bag.

The bedside light switch was still shaky; he would fix that first. Then he would wash down all the paintwork — anything to occupy himself. But, hell, this was bloody silly. He did not enjoy masochism. Perhaps Nikolai and his wife would put up with him for the night? Lev might even be with them — they could have another session, if Lyudmila would tolerate it.

He couldn't imagine why he had come here. If it hadn't been for the furniture, he would have stayed in barracks. Better that than enduring this morbid loneliness. He would be lucky to sell all the furniture *in situ* to the new tenant, another student. Alexei fumbled in his bag and brought out the vodka bottle he had bought at the store on his way; he poured himself a stiff slug.

That was better ... but his mind insisted on returning to the mess he had made. His father had not said so in as many words, but he was obviously bitterly disappointed in the path his son was following. 'It's a waste of a good brain,' he had said. 'You're drinking and smoking too much, son — and your marriage: that's no way to live.' Alexei had bridled but had remained silent. He had been away from home for four years and he was responsible for his own actions.

To hell with it — bugger this bloody joint. He kicked viciously at the empty bed with its bare mattress. He swallowed another slug and replaced the bottle in his bag. He flung on his coat and hurried from the flat.

A dusting of snow had powdered the entrance, but the shower had stopped. The stars sparkled in the bowl of the night. Alexei filled his lungs with the cold, clean air — but he wondered whether he'd gone too far with the alcohol. As he strode towards Nikolai's district, remorse smothered him again, obliterating rational thought. He would make for the Opera and cut across the Nevsky to reduce the distance. Perhaps he should phone Nikolai first? There would be a kiosk near the cathedral museum where the tourists gathered during the summer.

Kazansky Square was busy on this Saturday evening. The lights from the crawling traffic were like glow-worms in the dark. The well-to-do, bent against the wind that was whipping up the snow, perused the menus outside the restaurants.

Alexei fumbled for his diary. He had had the sense to note Nikolai's communal phone number, otherwise he would have had to find an information service kiosk — a soul-destroying ritual and useless because he could not provide the details that would be required by the woman official: forenames, surname, date of birth. The performance could take half an hour and could cost eight kopecks. He found a phone box at the corner of Kazansky Square.

There was no reply, but a woman finally answered and told him to wait. The phone went dead. Half an hour later, with fresh change, the same woman came again on the line. 'They're away for the weekend,' she said and hung up.

Alexei pushed out into the cold, the frustration and loneliness still gnawing at his soul. He would *not* return to the flat. He must get over this despair, find a cheerful bar. There were strings of welcoming lights on the other side of Kazansky Square. He would walk past the cathedral-museum entrance and follow the streets round. Stuffing his hands deep into the pockets of his uniform greatcoat, he began strolling towards this towering edifice that was one of Leningrad's tourist attractions: the cathedral of the Virgin of Kazan, from which the vast square took its name.

A little further on from the massive cathedral, he found another much smaller church where the coloured glass in the windows glowed from the dim lighting inside. A sung mass must be in progress here because, as he neared the entrance, he could hear the faint cadence of a choir. He paused to catch the pure sound filtering through the swing doors which were opening and shutting for the elderly folk who were entering in a steady stream. Alexei was halfway across the porticos, when, on impulse, he turned and climbed the steps. He had not been inside a church since his childhood, but it would be warm in there. He could listen to the choir before going on to drown his sorrows.

As he approached the swing doors, a shadow detached itself from one of the pillars. The grey-uniformed policeman, a large man with metal fillings in his front teeth, signalled Alexei to the shadows, out of earshot from the public.

'You from the Academy?'

'No — the New Entry Barracks.'

'Why d'you want to go in?' The KGB man stood astride, barring the way, thumbs crooked into his belt.

Alexei hesitated. 'What's it got to do with you?' he retorted. 'I'm a naval officer.'

The KGB policeman shifted his weight. He extracted a notebook from his pocket. 'I have my orders. Are you going to tell me why you want to go into the church?'

'I want to see what goes on, that's all. Any law against that?'

The man grunted and held out a hand. 'Your papers.'

Alexei fumed while he waited for the return of his new naval identity card. Then he pushed past the policeman, entering the church. The KGB man had picked up his walky-talky and was speaking into it.

CHAPTER SIX

Alexei paused in the centre aisle, uncertain of himself. The congregation, half-filling the church for the evening mass, was bunched towards the front, beneath the ornate pulpits. There was no seating in this church; he had wanted somewhere to sit in the warmth; somewhere to think things out and so perhaps rid himself of this guilt and depression.

Small chapels, dark and unwelcoming, each with its own icon, studded the sides of the church. Then to the right he noticed a chapel on its own, almost on a level with the steps of the main altar. Two candles were flickering on either side of its painted icon. As he tiptoed towards the gloom of the side aisles, the cloisters echoed to a chant which he dimly recognized.

Several obscure shapes were scattered about the benches in the chapel which, a microcosm of the church, provided an oasis from the main stream of worshippers. Below the diminutive altar, a cluster of candle-flames flickered in the gloom; the glow from the soft light touched the gilt inlay, emphasizing the rich colours in the enamel of the icon.

Finding a seat by the pillar, Alexei sat quite still, allowing the mysterious serenity of the place to seep into him.

He did not understand the Church calendar, only that the State spring holiday was not far off. Easter was a religious ceremony, he knew that, when the Christians filled their churches. The Orthodox Church of Mother Russia realized the spiritual power which the mystical symbolism of its services provided. Church services, where held, were still spectacles of pious splendour on high mass days: last year, the police had

had to quell a riot when a large gathering of young people tried to gate-crash the Easter mass in one Leningrad church.

Tonight, the atmosphere was very different. The anthem was expressing the poignant drama of the crucifixion: the pure treble of the choristers floated to the fluted vault, the chant reiterating again and again the words of the psalmist. Through the beauty of its simplicity, the ancient prose was emphasizing exquisitely the eternal message for mankind of the coming of its Saviour.

Except for this one icon, all the other altars, statues and icons seemed to be draped in black crepe. Alexei would never forget these candles — hundreds of them flickering before the icons, the only relief to the gloom in the aisles. The congregation moved like a restless sea, as elderly women (and occasionally, a young woman) threaded towards their favourite icon to place their candles.

Alexei felt utterly insignificant. Here he was, an atheistic young Russian, indoctrinated by the State to worship Lenin, spiritually numb, sitting alone in this beautiful church which belonged truly to the roots of his motherland. Here, he felt sure, reposed the soul of Russia; here the spirit that gave solace and perpetuity to the life of its people. The Party had done all it could do to exorcize the Christian religion from the lives of its young. By fostering contempt for the Christian credo, their masters had almost succeeded. 'It's for old women,' the Communists reiterated, 'and kids' stuff.' Alexei's generation, and those who had preceded him, were not bothered by religion.

And yet, why did man profoundly need his God? Why could the Party never extinguish this Christian faith? The KGB had given up with the older generation, but there seemed always to be more old women, as each generation progressed, streaming into the churches: always these old ladies whose patient eyes reflected with resignation the suffering of the faceless millions. They would be making their pilgrimage here for centuries to come, long after this political creed was replaced.

Alexei watched a hunched, birdlike figure, well into her eighties, tottering forwards, a candle clutched between her hands — and one more votive offering fluttered at the feet of the gentle Virgin. The Mother serenely contemplated the child lying woodenly in her lap; the royal-blue drapery of her mantle enshrined both head and shoulders in a line of flowing grace. The Virgin and her child — was this icon the Virgin of Kazan?

A young man edged past, carrying an unlit candle. He added his libation and another candle glowed, taller than the rest. When he turned, Alexei was surprised that he was only in his early thirties, moustachioed in the modern, Mexican style. Unselfconsciously, the man turned to kneel in prayer for a few seconds. Then he crossed himself and disappeared into the darkness of the aisle.

Alexei felt mentally exhausted; he had to force himself to concentrate for any length of time. But here, in the mystical atmosphere of the church, he became aware of the latent teachings which his parents had inculcated into him during his Tallin childhood, before the State got at him. Surely all these folk in the congregation could not be the simpletons which the Party claimed? His father, though he had never referred to it, was at his roots a believer — and he was no fool. His mother could more easily be expected to accept this faith: 'As the Jesuits say,' she once told him, 'give me a child until he is seven and the world can do what it likes.'

And sitting here, listening to the voices of the choristers lilting to the roof, Alexei felt a physical longing, an ache about his heart. He needed help, someone he could trust ... and for the first time in his life, he was consciously calling to this God whom, they said, was everywhere — but how did you reach Him?

All this symbolism, this dignified ceremony, was *not* so much hogwash. This was no meaningless ritual, but something alive in the realm of the spirit, something beyond comprehension which no genius in metaphysics could ever understand or explain. The fervour of one Christian; the simple, retiring nature of another; the purity and isolation through the struggle of choice of the priest and the nun — all these were dimensions which no 'Party man' could begin to understand. Without this indefinable spirit, man was at best an animal; at worst, an intelligent manipulator and controller of the human species.

These millions of voiceless people, strung across the republics and dancing to the central committee's tune — what had they to fear while they had Mother Church? And Mother Church, formerly one of Russia's greatest glories, was indestructible — tonight's experience was visible evidence, if proof were needed, after over sixty years of Communism.

Alexei's disastrous marriage; his selfishness with Maya, whom he had never tried to understand; the hunger of his body — none of these failures could be alleviated by the credo of the political system. Who cared, anyway? And if you made a mess of your life, what did it matter to them? Millions of other ants were ready to take your place — an endless trail leading to nowhere.

His pent-up emotion welled to the surface. The scalding tears spilled down his cheeks and he slid to his knees. He held his head between his hands, allowing the tears to stream, his silent sobbing racking his body in the darkness. '*God, oh, my God…*' The words tumbled from him in an agonized whisper

— he knew no prayers, had forgotten everything but a few words of the Lord's Prayer, as they called it.

Alexei knelt there, the voices from the congregation swelling to a crescendo, while the choir took up the anthem.

He was sitting, mercifully alone and unnoticed, in his corner; but he did not care if his weakness showed. He had come here, a helpless, insignificant speck in the cosmos; but now, in his abject admission of failure, somehow he had gained something which, before, he would have ridiculed. For the first time during these terrible weeks, he did not feel entirely alone.

The paean of the choir's praise was reaching its end, submerging him in a stream of sound, when he sensed a gentle pressure on his arm. He remained staring in front of him, ashamed of his wet cheeks. The pressure was repeated and he turned. A young woman, a shawl about her head, was sitting in the seat next to him. She, too, was staring at the candle flames, those pin-points of light which, through his tears, had become a galaxy of golden stars shimmering in the darkness.

He turned towards the icon again, waiting for his cheeks to dry. He did not move, did not attempt to dislodge the small hand that lay on the sleeve of his coat. He did not know how long they knelt there, he and this mysterious woman. He glanced once more at the Virgin with her Child; then slipped slowly back onto the bench, waiting for the woman to do the same.

The congregation had thinned as the mass drew to its close. The candles on the high altar were extinguished one by one. The woman remained on her knees, her hands clasped before her, waiting for the last candle to splutter down.

Alexei waited, he knew not how long, content to savour this serenity forever — but this emotional evacuation was as raw as his original ache of despair. He did not care. Perhaps this indefinable peace was the opiate for which men craved? He could not leave immediately, anonymously slipping from this stranger's life. She was sliding back onto the bench, but still she did not turn her head.

'Who are you?' Alexei's whispered question seemed sacrilegious in the stillness.

Then she was peering up at him, a pale, oval face, touched by the flickering glow from the dying candle flame: shadows were the eyes, a blur her mouth. 'I feel like an intruder,' she whispered. 'But I recognized you from where I was sitting. Forgive me, please. I thought you needed someone.'

The candle spluttered and snuffed out, its pungent vapours curling about the chapel.

'We met at The Combos. Katya Lazareva,' the woman said. She was still unrecognizable in her shawl, but she was talking softly and Alexei had to incline his head to catch her words.

'Katya Lazareva,' he repeated with disbelief. 'Lev's cousin. What are you doing here?'

'My parents are in trouble. They've left the city, so I'm on my own.'

'But why did you come here?'

She began talking quietly in the anonymity of the darkness. Alexei gently drew back the edge of her shawl so that he could see her face.

'I'm the intruder now,' he whispered. 'Are you in trouble — or just lonely?'

'I came here to resolve some questions. You see, we're Christian Jews. Father's visa for Israel has been refused. The policeman outside the entrance took my name when I came in, and they'll link it with the disappearance of my parents.' She was sobbing against his shoulder. 'It's so cruel, so dreadfully cruel.' She sniffed and wiped her face with the corner of her shawl. 'I'm better now. We're a fine pair, aren't we?'

They sat motionless, until they heard the padding of someone approaching from behind. 'You must go now, my children,' the church official said. The priest spoke kindly, his tall figure looming over them in the darkness. 'The Lord be with you.'

'Come, Katya, follow me.'

She rose abruptly and moved out to the side aisle. He caught up with her by the western doors. He stood in front of her, barring the way.

'Don't go,' he whispered.

The small head nodded, as she twitched the shawl closer about her. 'Stay close, please,' she whispered, 'until we get past the guard.'

Alexei took her hand and entwined her fingers through his. 'Come, then.'

The door swung shut behind them. They hesitated, listening to the snow whispering upon the steps. The tall shadow still stood by the pillar, motionless, watching them. The fresh snow scrunched beneath their feet as Alexei hastened Katya across the empty square. He did not glance back until they had reached the Maly Opera. They stopped and looked towards the church whose spire was lost in the silver mists. She sighed when she saw his relief that apparently they were not being followed.

Alexei tucked her hand into the pocket of his greatcoat, and they set out briskly across the city. They did not speak. Neither wished to be the first to shatter the spell of this most magical moment, but, too soon, they were stamping their feet outside the entrance to his block of flats.

The doorway light slanted across Katya, illuminating her expressive features and glowing eyes. Alexei pushed open the door for her and followed her inside.

CHAPTER SEVEN

'Reckon you've earned it, Number One,' the captain said as he and Slepak perused the signal which the radio supervisor had brought them on the bridge. 'It's two years since you first joined this old tub as our fourth officer, isn't it?'

'Yes, sir. Five months before you took over the *249*. I was an acting sub-lieutenant then, but I became a sub-lieutenant after six months, when I became third officer. Seems a long time ago.'

'Not so long as most — you became my number one less than a year ago, remember? One of the new scheme, weren't you?'

Alexei Slepak nodded. His university batch had been looked upon with suspicion by the older hands. It had been hard going, but the toughness of this job, out for six weeks off the northern approaches, wallowing about in bad weather, month-in, month-out during the winter, soon sorted out the men from the boys. It was what you were, rather than the number of stripes you carried on your sleeve, which counted.

'I'm going down to breakfast,' the captain announced. 'Let me know if the visibility shuts down any worse: I'll set a course for home if it does. We've been out here long enough. The British can keep their bloody platforms, as far as I'm concerned.'

Slepak watched the Old Man doing his famous trick down the ladder: one heave onto the handrails and he swooshed out of sight to his cabin below. Another hour to go before number two, the navigator and Slepak's deputy in the communications department, took over the watch at eight.

To Alexei Slepak, it seemed an age since he had joined this old girl. 'You never forget joining your first ship,' they said. He had finished top of his class at Leningrad and had been thankful to get to sea after those two years of intensive training. The first year had been an unforgettable experience, given up to basic seamanship and political theory; the second, more to his liking, was for theoretical training in electronic warfare as applied to communications — the reason he had been sent to this ship, intelligence collector GS *249*, one of the later *Mayak* class.

These modified *Mayaks* carried less gear than the larger and more modern *Primorye*-class vessels, but they were more similar to the first intelligence collectors (AGIs) whose trawler hulls gave them such excellent sea-keeping qualities — one reason why those who served in these *Mayaks* regarded them with such affection. The work of the original intelligence collectors (AGIs) had pioneered Gorshkov's modern navy.

'Switch to hand,' Alexei ordered. 'Half speed.'

The helmsman wound on the pitch control.

'Starboard fifteen. Bring her round to one-six-o.'

'One-six-o. Aye, aye, sir.'

Alexei spoke into the mouthpiece of the broadcast system: '*D'ye hear there*? The ship will be rolling heavily in two minutes' time.' There had been too many breakages recently — difficult to account for when *249* returned to base.

The ship was light after five weeks on patrol. She was down on her diesel fuel and, when beam-on to the sea, she rolled her guts out. Alexei watched her bows swinging across the horizon, and then she took a green one on the nose. He braced for the shock and ducked instinctively as the water showered across the bridge.

When *249* rode the top of the crests, the oil platform was just visible, the flames from the flare-booms crimson where they streamed in the wind. This nor'-westerly had been blowing for days now, one depression following another, but they were used to this weather in this terrible part of the world. Alexei would be thankful to reach port for a change of scene, after his long apprenticeship.

They had been valuable years: he had picked up more practical seamanship in a few months out here than in years in the lecture rooms — and now he had pride in himself as a seaman, the snug feeling of superiority which these men of the little ships felt over their opposite numbers in the big stuff — and that even included the destroyers, who did little more than show the flag and shadow the Western fleets.

'Course, sir, one-six-o.'

'Very good. Shift to automatic pilot.'

He doubted whether the old girl would steer well enough on 'George' in this following sea. She had nearly broached several nights ago in that hooley, so they had kept her 'in hand' more than formerly. She was surging down the lee of the waves, the horizon invisible as she reached the troughs of the swell walloping in from the Atlantic. Alexei preferred *249* in these seas over all the bigger, more modern *Primoryes*.

He hoped the Old Man would exploit the opportunity which this bad weather gave them to quit the area half a day early — but their relief ship, another *Mayak*, had not yet signalled her position, so *249* would have to be patient. Since those British trawlers had passed during the night, the plot had been blank and uninteresting — there had been only the routine chatter from the Sulisker platform; and the trawlers fishing off Iceland, who were speaking in code to their owners in Fleetwood and Hull. That was all. The last week had been boring to a degree, unlike their last patrol when they had shadowed the British Fleet exercises west of the Faeroes.

The Royal Navy had maintained radio silence until the last moment, when they had obligingly saturated the ether with every sort of conceivable signal in plain language. Alexei still thought it had been a leg-pull for the benefit of the Russian intelligence collectors in the area: *249* had good monitoring gear, both in radio and radar, but she had been unable to cope that day. The new *Okeans* might have succeeded, but Alexei doubted it.

'How's she steering, quartermaster?'

'All right, sir. I couldn't do better in this.'

'We'll come down a bit. 140 revolutions.'

The chugging of the exhausts through the funnel decreased. The wind seemed to blow stronger from aft as her speed reduced, and the exhaust fumes around the bridge became obnoxious. Alexei moved across to the captain's phone.

'I've come round, sir. Course 160°, speed ten knots.'

'Very good. When the navigator comes up, tell him to work out a course for home. There's nothing doing today — it's the weekend, when our wicked capitalists are out enjoying themselves.'

'Right, sir. You asked me to grant a week's leave to each watch when we get in. When can I bring you the lists?'

'When you like. I'm working on my report.'

Alexei Slepak had been a sub-lieutenant (*leytenant*) for eighteen months. He could not expect rating up to full lieutenant (*starshiy leytenant*) for a while yet, but the promotion would help financially when it came. He moved out to the port wing and strolled round to the after side of the bridge. He could spend a few moments here, for the helmsman was a reliable hand and there was nothing about, even on the radar plot. Dawn had broken, and the sun might break through the cloud later on.

Alexei longed to see Leningrad again. These grey, dreary ports in the Kola inlet — he had seen enough of them to last a lifetime. He would be leaving *249* at Severomorsk and never wanted to see the place again. After a two-day handover to a chap he did not know two courses below him, he would take the night train for Vologda, where he would have to wait two hours for the Leningrad connection. A rotten journey, but Katya would be waiting for him at the end of it. He could see her now, his own Katenka, in her flared, suede-leather coat with the white fur collar, waiting for him at the barrier, as she had done on the last occasion he had rushed south for leave.

The ensign was fouled around its staff: he would have to send the bosun's mate down to clear it. The Old Man was a stickler for detail, insisting on a taut ship. It was these details which kept the crew on its toes — and so made *249* an efficient and happy vessel.

Katya Lazareva ... the future Mrs Slepak? Alexei grinned to himself as he leaned across the after rail. The molly birds were drifting across the stern, wheeling and tumbling with the wind, skimming the troughs while they waited for the breakfast gash to be ditched. He felt a sudden exultation at the thought of next week's meeting with Katenka — only nine days to go now — two days ought to be long enough for the handover, if his successor was not too much of a stickler for detail. The stores' inventory, and particularly the provisions, took the time.

He wondered what Katya would be looking like now. It was difficult to recall her features — hers was a mobile, elusive face and the photograph he had of her did not do her justice. She was a tough, restless woman, with swept-back, black hair like a boy's. Her superb legs, fine ankles and tiny feet carried a trim little body. She had been everything to him (and he to her, if she were telling the truth) following their incredible meeting in the church. Their love for each other had been total. Nothing could explain it — only that the feeling between them had grown into something almost too strong for either of them.

After their first night together, life had never been the same again: they had snatched at every moment to be together — she had even come up north to spend a weekend with him in Severomorsk. The journey had cost them both three months' savings, but every rouble had been worth it. In spite of the fearful difficulties which Katya's parents were encountering, from the first moment they had tried not to be censorious and had welcomed Alexei into their household — difficult for them, when he had still been officially married.

The divorce had come through last December. Maya had never mentioned a child, so she must have stuck to her decision to have it aborted. Alexei tried to shake off the memory of that terrible, soulless parting. He hoped she was happier now and may even have married again.

Four years, almost to the day, since he had joined. He would be twenty-six next month — still young enough to qualify for command, if he won his promotion shortly. He had, he realized now, been mentally unwell when he had joined. That had not been the fault of the navy. His depression had been a nightmare, but he had shaken it off eventually — and he had enjoyed those years of training. He wondered to what ship he would be appointed next, once he had left dear old *249*. He had better return to the wheelhouse.

He heard the captain's distinctive cough as he clambered up the ladder. Alexei stood by the compass, checking the ship's head. 'George' was coping with the seas, thank heavens.

'The platform's out of sight, sir. There's nothing about.'

The captain was handing him a scrap of paper. 'Thought you'd like to see this,' he said. 'It's your lucky day.'

'To GS *249* from C-in-C, Leningrad,' Alexei read. 'Sub-Lieutenant Slepak promoted to Lieutenant from the first of June. Officer to proceed on leave to await further appointment. He is to report home address.' Alexei looked up and smiled.

'All right, Number One...' the Old Man grunted. 'I'd better do my good deed for the day too. Tell the navigator to come up. It's time we were off, back to base.'

CHAPTER EIGHT

From here, in her usual place on the stairway leading to the station restaurant, Katya could watch the passengers disgorging from the Vologda express. Unshaven men; mothers hauling heavy-eyed children along by the hand; the passengers were crowding at the barriers — and then she saw Alexei, his hand waving above the heads of the crowd. She skipped down the steps and mingled with the others who had also risen early to meet the train.

Her own Alexei — what more could she want? His face was burnt by the wind and the cold. She always felt this jolt of pleasure when first she saw him after any length of time: she flung herself into his arms, clinging to him, burying her head in his chest, uncertain that this was reality. When she met him after these separations, he always looked larger than she remembered: she had forgotten how broad his shoulders were, how narrow his hips. 'Alyosha, my Alyoshenka...' she whispered.

Katya picked up two of his cases and led the way to the cab rank. Her head on his shoulder in the back of the taxi, she told him of her father's offer. 'He is insisting that we use their flat for a few days while they take some time off. He'll be asking you at breakfast.' She was watching him from the corner of her eye, while he stared at the green of the park flashing past the window.

'I thought we were going camping down in Tallin? We could find a site by the banks of the Pirita. My parents used to take me there as a kid.'

'You'd rather get away — not use their flat?'

'It's kind of them, but I want you all to myself. I've dreamed about it for so long. We can hire all the gear when we get there.' Alexei smiled down at her, then added, 'But we mustn't hurt their feelings, they've been so good to us. Your father could have made life impossible for us both — he need not have accepted me. He's trusted me throughout his ordeal, in spite of my being an NO — and presumably a Party man.'

Katya stiffened and peered into those blue eyes. 'You still haven't become a member?'

'No, Katenka, I haven't. That's all they have against me. The captain gave me a good report.'

The taxi slowed, then swung right, across the Nevsky. 'Nearly home,' Katya murmured. 'Here we are, dear old Lomonosov Street. Number 52,' she called to the driver. 'Just past the chemist.'

In the lift, she kissed Alexei fully on the lips. 'We're going camping,' she whispered. 'We'll catch the 11.56.'

But her dad was persistent at breakfast, and it was only Alexei's tact that turned the corner. 'Okay,' Mr Lazarev had said, giving up. 'Let's hope you have good weather. What address are you giving Admiralty?'

Katya felt the silence falling between them, the young naval officer with his rigid training, and the ageing scientist whose searching mind knew no boundaries. He glanced at her mother, who then said: 'It's too dangerous, Alexei, to give them our address — just when things are quietening down.'

Alexei put his arm about the frail, grey-haired woman. 'We'll find a site and phone through our address. No problem.'

Katya left the table, as the conversation turned to Alexei's life at sea during the past months. She would pack a bag for each of them. She'd have to hurry, if they were to catch this train — and she must not forget the swimming things.

'I'll never forget today, Alex,' Katya said softly. 'Everything's gone our way for a change.' She put her arm about his waist, as in silence they watched the sunset. The path of the sun sparkled rose and gold upon the surface of the sea; at their feet the Pirita glided to the Baltic, which was screened by the line of trees on the other bank. The last of the birdsong stilled. The scent of the pines wafted on the air, as twilight turned to night.

'We were lucky to find this spot,' Alexei murmured. 'They told me this was the best site — one of the few on its own.'

'Worth every kopek.' Katya stood close to him, enchanted by the peace of the evening. 'Need anything else to eat?' They had shared their supper beneath the pines, a simple meal with a bottle of Georgian wine Alexei had bought at the camp store.

'I'm not hungry.' He drew her down to the soft, pine-needled bank and began unbuttoning her blouse. Katya lay supine while his eyes wandered slowly over her.

'It's my turn,' she whispered, peeling off his shirt.

The final flush of the sinking sun touched the pines, caressed the curve of his shoulder, tinged his fair hair where he lay propped on one elbow, gazing down at her. Katya watched him through half-closed lids, trying to lock this second in her memory forever … and she shivered suddenly as a strange, chilling presentiment swept over her that perhaps they would never again share such a perfect moment. They were out of the world for a few idyllic hours: tomorrow Alexei would be contacting Admiralty, and then he would no longer be entirely hers, not as he was now, during this night beneath the stars. The light had already faded, and she could see only the outline of his body against the deepening sky.

'It's getting chilly,' Katya whispered. Alexei drew the blouse about her shoulders; then he picked her up and carried her to the tent, where he laid her on the sleeping bag. 'Come quickly, my Alyosha,' she whispered, 'the whole night's ours.' She touched his wide lips with her fingertips. Outside, through the darkening rectangle of the tent door, a pair of nightingales pierced the stillness of the night with their limpid song.

Katya and Alexei had wanted to talk afterwards — to discuss the events that were altering their lives, to make the decisions they must make. But they had fallen asleep, and now Katya did not know what had happened to the night. The nightingales had ceased; in the moonlight, the shadows of the pine branches traced filigree patterns across the fabric of the tent. She lay still, loath to glance at his watch which he had placed on top of their clothes by her side. She stroked his back where he lay across her, his head between her breasts. He stirred, then awoke, his hands moving over her.

'My beloved Katenka, what's to become of us? I can't live without you.'

'Shh … you've got me now. I'll never leave you … never.'

'What'll you do if your father's visa comes through?'

'Later, darling. We'll talk about that later.' Katya fought against the worldly things, the terrible, manmade barriers that people forged for each other. Tonight, she longed only to surrender herself to Alexei; to capitulate utterly to his lovemaking. Whatever befell in the future, they could hold this night locked in their souls for the rest of time.

Time merged into eternity as they surrendered to the flood that overwhelmed them. Then she lay, head on his shoulder, as they whispered together in the moonlight.

'Will you go with them,' Alexei asked softly, 'if they are allowed out to Israel?'

During these last years, Katya had often wrestled with the terrible decision that she knew she might have to make someday. Yet, with the moment upon her, she allowed her instinct to speak for her. 'It depends on you,' she said.

'What d'you mean?' Alexei leant on his elbow, looking down at her, the steel glinting in his eyes. 'You'll stay with me, even if your parents go?'

Katya nodded and brushed his forearm with her lips. 'I'd rather we could *all* settle out there — start a new life in Israel. That's all I pray for.'

'But if I was killed? If I died before then?'

The question was too brutal, here beneath the moon and in each other's arms. She remained silent, rigid beneath him. 'I don't think about it often. But if … if…' Her voice fell to a whisper again. 'I'd follow them out, as soon as I could. I couldn't stay here, not if that happened.'

They did not speak, but lay there, listening to the breeze soughing through the pines. 'Dawn's breaking,' Alexei said, lowering himself upon her. He fell asleep, her hands about his head.

Katya lay awake, gently ruffling his hair when the first light crept into the sky. Soon this paradise would reach its abrupt end; Alexei would be off again, leaving her alone, awaiting a future which might never manifest. She must have dozed off, for she was dimly aware that a bell was ringing from the direction of the camp office. The sun was already drenching their tent in light.

They went down to the beach for their lunch. Alexei had wasted two hours trying to get through to Admiralty, so he had finally despatched a telegram giving the campsite's address.

Katya cherished these precious days. They spent the mornings lazing on the beach, the afternoons whiling away the time by walking the countryside. They were charmed by the ruins of the convent of Saint Brigitte, a memorial to the days when man's spirit counted for more than the materialism of this age. Hand-in-hand, time became meaningless as they shared their regrets and began to discover each other's innermost thoughts. Katya talked of her family, of how she had been brought up after her parents had become Christian Jews. They dreamed their dreams, shared their secret hopes for the future.

There was nothing they could do to halt time while Professor Lazarev waited for his visa. Alexei would persevere with his career; Katya would meet him when she could: her secretarial job was temporary and she could get away easily. They would marry as soon as he was promoted to lieutenant-commander (*kapitan leytenant*), hopefully in three years' time. The second night merged into the third day, the third into the fourth; they had discovered a peak of happiness which neither had dreamed could exist.

And the weather blessed their heaven — the sun poured down on them, so they spent their time swimming and lying on the hot sand. On the fifth morning they walked to Kadriorg, where they picnicked on cold chicken, raspberries and wine. In the afternoon they wandered back to the beach, where they swam and slept until the shadows lengthened across the sands. Then they gathered up their things and strolled towards their backwater by the banks of the Pirita. They were passing the office when a young woman approached them.

'There's a message from Leningrad,' she said. 'They want you to call this number.'

They, *they* ... always those mysterious, faceless officials juggling with people's lives, as if they were numbers in the

State's computerized lottery. Katya had wandered alone back to the tent. She had known, before she watched Alexei walking slowly back towards her, that her woman's intuition had not failed her.

'They've recalled me,' he said simply. 'I've got to report immediately to Room 604, Admiralty. They want me back tonight.'

CHAPTER NINE

Captain Petrovich rose from his desk in Office 604 of the Admiralty building in Leningrad. 'We'll soon see if Slepak's as good as his reports indicate,' he said, turning to his deputy, Lieutenant-Commander Panov. 'He's on his way up now.' Both men were political officers, and both were overworked, particularly since this bother with *Uranus*: the affair was reflecting badly upon the political department. The incident stemmed from the original appointment of that feeble man, Vilms, *Uranus*'s commissar. He should have been retired years ago — and Captain Petrovich guessed that Panov had come to the same conclusion.

Panov said, 'Things should get better, sir, so long as Slepak gets on with the new commissar, Commander Grenz. He finished his takeover last week. I've sent Vilms on indefinite leave.'

'Grenz is a hard man, the sort of Commissar *Uranus* needs. Slepak will *have* to get on with him.'

'And with his captain, sir. Captain Lessner isn't all that easy, I gather.'

'We've got no positive evidence yet about Captain Lessner,' Petrovich added. 'I'm hoping that Slepak can smooth things out quickly — we've more important things on our plate than *Uranus*.'

'The intelligence boys get too big for their boots sometimes, sir.'

Captain Petrovich nodded. 'Let Slepak in, will you?' The red indicator was blinking at the side of Petrovich's desk. The door opened and he glanced up at the lieutenant saluting before him. 'Sit down, Slepak. Lieutenant-Commander Panov is my assistant.'

Slepak took off his cap and sat in the chair alongside Panov — they could observe him from both angles. Petrovich touched the recording button beneath the lip of his desk.

'I've recalled you from leave because they tell me you know something about small ships and the way they work. We've had good reports on you.'

'Thank you, sir.' The man spoke guardedly — understandable, under the circumstances. He had a humorous face, and it was evident why he had been reported on as a 'good mixer'. Perhaps his direct entry from university had something to do with his apparent maturity?

'Sorry I had to curtail your leave, but something important has turned up.'

'It's confidential,' Panov added. 'You're under oath not to divulge a word of this interview to anyone, Slepak. No one, d'you understand?'

The lieutenant nodded. He might have shown a bit more interest, more respect, Petrovich thought. He went on: 'We were going to send you on your "long" electronic warfare course, because you've been recommended. But you'll have to wait until you've finished this job for us. If you wrap it up quickly, as I'm sure you will, I'll see your promotion doesn't suffer.'

Slepak was showing more animation. 'Thank you, sir.' Again, that touch of sarcasm — no one appreciated their leave being cut short.

'As Lieutenant-Commander Panov has said, this interview is a delicate matter, so what I have to tell you *must* remain secret. I shall know at once if you divulge a word of our conversation.'

'Of course, sir.'

The captain drummed his fingertips upon the desktop. '*Uranus* is down in Sevastopol, attached to C-in-C, Black Sea Fleet. I need a new first lieutenant for her.'

The muscles in Slepak's face tautened.

'Her number one's gone sick,' Panov added. 'They've had to take him out of the ship without relief. Their number two's taking the weight until you join her.'

'What was wrong with my predecessor, sir?' Slepak asked, ignoring Panov.

'Some mental instability, I believe,' Petrovich replied, glancing across at his assistant. 'That's right, isn't it?'

'He's in hospital, sir.'

Petrovich smiled disarmingly — a different approach was necessary with Slepak. 'I've selected you, Lieutenant, because I need someone with intelligence.' He smiled again. 'The ship is not as efficient as she should be — we can't all be good number ones. Her commissar was a bit old for the job.' The message was sinking in — Slepak had folded his arms, was more erect in the chair. 'NATO's Mediterranean exercises are due next month. It's your job to work *Uranus* to full efficiency before she sails. You've got the new commissar to help you: Commander Grenz.'

'He joined ten days ago,' Panov said. 'A live wire.'

Petrovich wished that Panov could leave the interview to him — he'd dress him down afterwards. He pushed the cigarettes across to Slepak.

'No thank you, sir. Is my captain in the picture?' Slepak's blue eyes were difficult to meet.

'Not entirely: it would not be fair on him. That's one reason why I want you to treat this interview confidentially. You must shake up the ship and help the captain all you can.'

'Do I know him, sir? Was he ever in the Northern Fleet?'

Petrovich smiled his condescension. 'I think not. He was my term — one of the senior commanders in the intelligence service: Captain Lessner.' He paused and regarded the officer sitting before him. Slepak might match up all right. 'You'll be joining *Uranus* tomorrow. You've made his travelling arrangements, Panov?'

'Eight-thirty flight tomorrow morning, sir. I've got him a bed for the night in the wardroom.'

Slepak seemed tense, his mouth compressed in a thin line of obstinacy. 'I've got one or two things to do, sir. May I make my own arrangements for tonight? I can find my own way to the airport in the morning.' Petrovich detected the anxiety in the innocent question.

'Your leave's been cancelled. There's nothing I can do about it now.' Petrovich was watching the man's reaction. 'There's one other thing, Slepak: I see from your record that you have so far been unable to join the Party. I look to you to rectify that omission.' He smiled bleakly, then turned to Panov. 'And what was the other matter, Panov?' He flipped a cigarette from the packet and flicked the lighter. Slepak had turned towards Panov, the muscles working in his cheek.

'Lieutenant…' Panov, at his most aggressive, had fixed Slepak with that insolent stare. 'As political officers, we have to know everything that is going on. Commander Grenz will be reporting back to us. That's his job — on the captain downwards. D'you understand?'

Slepak nodded, then rose in silence from the chair and reached for his cap.

'One moment, Slepak. Lieutenant-Commander Panov has rightly told you that it is our job to supervise morale: we keep a dossier on everyone. We're particularly sensitive to the contacts which naval officers maintain with civilians.'

'Naturally, sir.'

Petrovich tapped his fingertips together. 'You know a Professor Lazarev?'

The alarm signal was definitely flickering in Slepak's eyes.

'And his family — his daughter?'

'Yes, sir. I've met them.'

Petrovich stared from behind his desk. He leaned across to select the correspondence from the 'In' basket. 'That's all, Lieutenant. Carry on. Lieutenant-Commander Panov will take you to the transport officer.'

CHAPTER TEN

Katya knew, before she picked up the phone, that it would be Alexei.

'That you, Katenka?'

'Yes, Alyosha. What's wrong?'

The line hummed. Then he said: 'I can't see you tomorrow — that's all.'

'Can you tell me?' The urge to ask the question, to eradicate the doubts flooding her mind was irresistible.

'Nothing's altered between us.' She could hardly hear him. 'D'you understand, Katenka? Nothing's changed … nothing. Bye.'

The phone went dead. Katya sat on the settee, too numbed to speak; the tears began coursing down her cheeks.

'My poor child.' She felt an arm about her shoulder as her mother led her to the bedroom.

Through the haze of the sleeping pill, Katya heard the shrill of the phone again. Though the alarm clock showed 11.40, her mother was up and taking the call. 'It's for you, Katya,' she was saying.

She scrambled from her bed. Her mother whispered: 'He won't say who he is.'

'Miss Katya Lazareva?'

'Yes. Katya speaking. Who's that?'

'I'm a friend of a friend of yours.' The man was barely audible, his speech clipped and decisive. 'He can't contact you himself; he's asked me to phone you.'

The warning signals were flashing in her brain. 'Yes?' She hesitated. 'Who are you, please?'

'Pirita,' the anonymous voice murmured. 'He said you'd understand... Pirita.'

'Is he all right?'

'He's okay. Airport tomorrow at seven — by the inquiries desk.'

'I'll be there. Tell him that.' The phone clicked.

Katya's father was standing by her. 'Take the car,' he said. 'I don't need it — you'll be better on your own.'

She set the alarm and crawled back to bed. Her mother came in and kissed her. 'Don't worry about oversleeping,' she said. 'I'll wake you.'

The hanging clock in the airport's vast hall showed 6.50. Katya stood, hesitating between the automatic glass doors, when a tall figure in naval uniform strode past her. Alexei did not turn his head, but his eyes, tired in his pale face, told her all she needed. She let him draw ahead, before following him through the exit doors to the forecourt outside. He was scrutinizing a brochure, waiting for her to lead the way. She walked quickly past him and made for the carpark. She climbed into the little Zaporozhet (the mini-car for which her dad had had to pay cash on the nail, after waiting three years for delivery) and waited for Alexei. She pushed open the door as he came level.

'Drive to the main park,' he murmured, gazing unconcernedly in front of him. 'We can talk there. I've got fifty minutes.'

Katya found the compound and parked in a corner, well screened by overnight parkers.

Alexei held her in silence, staring down at her. She traced the outline of his face with her fingertips while he recounted the disastrous developments of the last twenty-four hours.

'I've told you everything, Katenka,' he blurted in conclusion. 'Duty's a bloody hard taskmaster.'

'We've a duty to be happy, too,' she added gently. 'How long d'you think you'll be away?' She had not meant to trouble him: the lines about his mouth were tense, his eyes sunken.

'When I've finished this *Uranus* job, they'll send me on my long course. They promised me that.'

'Back here, in Leningrad?'

Alexei nodded and kissed her roughly, crushing her to him. 'If we're in Sevastopol for any length of time, why don't you come down, if we can find a job for you? They're always looking for secretaries.'

The time had slipped from them. 'Don't wait to see me off,' he had whispered after their silent walk back to the departure desk. 'And may our God take care of us.' He did not look back. Katya watched his upright figure, a bag slung from each arm, filtering through the control.

She walked up to the observation lounge overlooking the aircraft park. She caught a glimpse of him mingling with the other passengers queueing up for the boarding ladder into the TU-144. She blocked her ears from the scream of its jets, as it circled slowly towards the distant runway.

She remained there, steeling herself for her last sight of the machine that was to snatch him 1,700 kilometres away from her. Then it came lumbering down the runway, parallel to the airport buildings. The blast from the jets struck the building. The nose of the aircraft rose and then the TU-144 was airborne and climbing into the dawn. Katya watched its shallow turn; she remained staring at the trail staining the sky until long after his aircraft had disappeared. That vanishing puff of smoke was the last evidence that these few days had been more than a dream: he and she were indivisible now, whatever the distance, whatever fate had lurking for them. She turned her back and walked briskly back to find her father's car.

For his sake she would drive carefully, and ignore the temptation to drive the Zaporozhet into the nearest wall. 'My Alyosha,' she whispered. 'They can't take you away now — never.' And then she realized that he had told her everything. She must never let a word of it slip, not even to her parents.

Alexei was glad to have found this half-hour, up here on the clifftop overlooking Sevastopol harbour. He needed a moment to collect himself — lunchtime was not the most opportune moment for a first lieutenant to join his ship. He had left his bags with the police at the main gate and had retained the taxi to bring him here. The walk back would do him good and would take only half an hour, if he entered the dockyard by that northern gate, the nearest to North Corner, where *Uranus* lay among the smaller ships at Number 17 jetty. As he had driven past in the taxi, he had caught sight of the AGIs huddled together on their own.

The TU-144 had landed on time. He could not remember much about the flight, unremarkable as it had been at 9,000 metres. The emotion he had suffered on parting from Katya had drained him dry. He had sat with his eyes closed until the numbness had passed. He had not cared whether this silver bullet had disintegrated into oblivion. When the plane began its descent, he had forced himself to face the imminence of reality. He had a job to do: the better he did it, the sooner they could be together again.

The hot breeze on the clifftop was sweeping away his tiredness. The magnificent harbour of Sevastopol lay stretched at his feet, a mirror of blue water on this summer's day. The surface danced with mirage where the big ships lay, swinging haphazardly to their moorings. It must have been very different during the Great Patriotic War, when only the gaunt fingers of rusting funnel tops, masts and rigging broke the surface of the harbour. The plaque and the photographs on the memorial had recorded those days only too vividly: Sevastopol had played its part no less heroically than what was once Stalingrad. The port had been overrun by the enemy, fought over, and finally liberated by the Red Army. The Germans had been halted here, but not without fearful cost: no house had been left standing; strings of railway wagons had dangled from these clifftops. You'd never recognize Sevastopol now, from those wartime photographs.

The ships seemed like toy boats where they swung to their moorings, or lay at their jetties. C-in-C, Black Sea, had his headquarters here and the power of the Mediterranean Task Force was easily recognizable: those VTOL carriers, the *Kurils*, were as modern as any in the world. Their presence, showing the flag around the globe, had more than compensated for their cost.

This naval base served the bulk of the surface ships, the submarines being at Balaclava, further down the coast between here and Yalta. Tucked into this North Corner were the little ships, the 'chars' who worked incessantly for their mistresses the cruisers, the new carriers and the destroyer boys. There, at his feet, were the AGIs, the sweepers, the survey ships and the landing craft in their rectangular ugliness. There were destroyers, frigates and, separated from their larger cousins, several FACs (Fast Attack Craft), presumably en route to their base at Novorossiysk.

The cranes and huge workshops of the dockyard merged with the city: Alexei could see on the far side of the base the complex of the C-in-C's offices and the landing stages for the fleet's boats. It was time to leave: the hands would be turning-to for the afternoon and he would join as the afternoon's work was getting underway. He felt a foreboding: either because he was joining a new ship for the first time as a first lieutenant, or because of this ship's reputation, he did not know. Whatever the reason, he would insist on his own discipline as quickly and as unobtrusively as he dared.

Lieutenant Slepak sat in his shirtsleeves in his cabin, slumped in his chair, his arms crossed behind his head. He had just ticked off on his calendar the seventeenth day since joining *Uranus*. It was already past one o'clock in the morning; he had promised himself an early night, but he would collect his thoughts before turning in. He *must* mentally stand back for a moment to make sure he was on the right lines, because events were not going as he had hoped. They had been correct in Leningrad: things weren't right in *Uranus*.

Alexei had seen her for the first time when the dockyard transport had dumped him with his bags at North Corner. *Uranus* was the inboard AGI on the trot. He had been searching for a ship below standard, but she was even scruffier than he had imagined. Her ensign was fouled around the staff, a rope's end hung over her port quarter and a couple of capless seamen in dirty overalls were skulking behind the after screen. Rusting scratch-lines showed along her side, amidships; her once white upperworks were streaked grey with dirt and patches of rust showed about her bridge superstructure.

Another *Moma* was the outboard ship on the trot: she looked 'taut' in comparison, her superstructure gleaming white, her hands properly dressed and working energetically. No one was at the head of *Uranus*'s skewed gangway when Slepak walked on board for the first time.

That first day had been only an example of what lay ahead. He had met the captain, Felix Lessner; the 'number two' and navigating officer, Lieutenant Marc Klavitter; and the political officer, Commander Karl Grenz, in that order, during the first hour. The others he had encountered in the wardroom at supper.

It was all a blur now, but he had tried not to judge his fellow officers on first impressions. Only after this interval could he begin to assess them: he had time for the doctor, Nikolai Bogoraz, who was the same age as himself; and the electrical officer, Lieutenant Georgiy Baugersky, but the remainder seemed a very mixed bag. Karl Grenz was a loner and obviously a dedicated commissar.

As first lieutenant of *Uranus*, Slepak was in charge of the communications department, the largest section in the ship — eighteen ratings, including the Chief Radio Electrical Artificer, Litke, who ran the department efficiently. The third hand, Acting Sub-Lieutenant Valeriy Perstev, twenty-three years old, was divisional officer of the communications department. He had already demonstrated to Alexei his thick-skinned tactlessness and buffoonery when dealing with the ratings.

The fourth hand, a callow youth of twenty-two, Roman Surov, acting sub-lieutenant, helped the navigating officer. This man, Klavitter, was twenty-five, due for promotion, and had been holding the weight as first lieutenant while waiting for their new number one to join. He did not hide his disappointment that he had not been rated up as *Uranus*'s new first lieutenant.

Slepak had not been impressed with his first meeting with the captain. Captain Felix Lessner tried too hard to please. All smiles and charm, he had lounged in his armchair, dispensing optimism. He was the captain, he had said: he liked things the way they were. If he, Slepak, wanted to change anything, he, the captain, would want to know about it. He was a tall man, still lean and tough, though in his middle forties. His ruddy, leathery face was spoilt by a bad tempered, slack mouth and his brown eyes brooded with resentment. Alexei suspected he was unsure of himself; behind that facade of bonhomie lurked a man who needed reassurance and wanted to be liked. He was a mystery as yet, and Alexei felt ill at ease with him. He did not refer to his family; the only photo on his desk was that of a young girl of about twelve years old. Though their first meeting had been at three in the afternoon, Lessner had insisted on downing a tot to welcome Slepak's arrival.

On his second day, Slepak had gathered the officers together in the wardroom. 'We'll paint the ship tomorrow,' he said. 'I'll clear lower deck, except for the engine room department.' He smiled across at the chief, Engineer-Lieutenant Maxim Melvedev, two years his senior in age. 'You have your hands full in the engine room, haven't you, Chief?'

'You can say that again, Number One — and since when has the engine room department been expected to help out the upper deck paint ship?'

The ensuing silence had angered Alexei. He abruptly ordered all officers to muck in too, to help paint ship when lower deck was cleared on the following morning. He had sensed the resentment when he dismissed the meeting. It was evident that a chasm existed between wardroom and messdeck that no one cared to cross. Alexei proposed to remedy the fault once and for all — the hands would see that *Uranus*'s appearance concerned everyone on board.

Commissar Grenz had remained aloof. Apart from a curt greeting to Alexei on his first day, Grenz had encountered Slepak only when passing on the upper deck — he ate with the captain in the commanding officer's cabin. But that 'paint-ship' forenoon had changed everything — Slepak had registered that unlucky incident as the start of much of the later trouble.

'Paint-ship' was going well: the weather was fine, the painter had done his stuff the night before, and the paint was mixed and ready; the pots were burnt-off and clean; the seamen had already slung the stages over the side. The CREA, Litke, had set an example by encouraging his hands to slap on the white paint rapidly, all about his radio rooms. A couple of volunteers had previously been sent aloft to wash down the dirty mast, and soon it was beginning to gleam with fresh, white paint. It was the radio operator, Arbatov, wrapped around the DF aerial, who dropped his pot.

Commander Grenz was working on his papers in the cool of the after bridge. He was sitting on his camp stool, crouched over a folding table when the disaster struck. The pot missed him, but his summer uniform and his papers were splattered. In the shocked silence, a sailor guffawed from the next ship.

Grenz had taken the accident as a personal affront; after first lieutenant's defaulters the next morning, Grenz had assumed that Alexei's refusal to take the case on to the captain was a challenge to the commissar's authority. He had persuaded the captain to summon his number one and to insist that the offender be brought before the captain's table. The young RO had been punished harshly by the Old Man: this had been Alexei's first encounter with Lessner's volatile behaviour.

Slepak's relations with Grenz had begun wretchedly: the commissar had sent for Alexei and, during the heat of that same afternoon, had lectured him on discipline. Keeping Slepak standing, Commissar Grenz had stalked up and down his minute cabin.

'You may be the first lieutenant aboard *Uranus*,' the political officer had fumed, 'but I'll have you remember, Slepak, that you are also responsible to me, as well as to your captain.' Alexei had held his tongue while he watched this barrel-chested, short-arsed, humourless man stomping to-and-fro across the cabin. The man was a menace, a mini computer who forgot nothing once his evil little mind was made up. His grey-green eyes were darting suspiciously beneath the sandy eyebrows. His thinning hair was brushed carefully across the balding head which glistened, as did his smooth cheeks, in the sweltering cabin. His thick arms swung jerkily, his hand gesticulating, as he worked himself into a lather. His metal-capped teeth showed through half-opened lips as he blustered in his high-pitched monotone — and when he passed close to Alexei, his breath had smelt foul. Alexei had kept his temper only by reminding himself of the Admiralty interview in Leningrad. Grenz, he felt sure, sensed that Alexei had been put in the picture by higher authority.

Slepak had carried out messdeck rounds on his second night on board. He had accompanied the officer-of-the-day, Perstev, and had asked the coxswain, Chief Petty Officer Korolev, at forty the oldest rating in the ship, to introduce the leading hands of the messes. The silence in the messdecks had been unnerving. On the next day, Alexei had sent for the ship's company records. Their study had kept him awake till the small hours, but the effort had been worth it. What he had learned, he had kept to himself.

Even after this short time, he felt that some of the tension might be easing. True, Grenz hated his guts; number two's jealousy was only too apparent in his sarcastic replies to Alexei's questions; Perstev was also hostile, though afraid of the first lieutenant's authority; Melvedev, the chief, went his own way in the engine room — and yet the 'buffer' (the petty officer in charge of the upper deck), Petty Officer Vritsky, seemed less offhand and was becoming more co-operative. He had ceased his 'We didn't do it like this before, sir.' Some of the hands, too, particularly in Litke's department, were showing by their efforts that they realized that at last something positive was happening to their ship.

Alexei's self-inflicted loneliness had not bothered him. He had worked to exhaustion, trying to dull the pain of separation. He had received one letter from Katya — and, between the lines, she was as lonely as he was. He would nip ashore next week and try to telephone her. He rose from his chair and drew back the coverlet of his bunk. Then he heard a faint tapping on his cabin door.

CHAPTER ELEVEN

Surgeon-Lieutenant Nikolai Bogoraz closed the cabin door behind him. He turned, his eyes wary behind his rimless spectacles. 'It's a bit late, Number One,' he apologized. 'I saw your light was still on. Cigarette?'

The doctor seemed tense. Only the quartermaster was on deck; the wardroom had turned in hours ago.

'Take my chair, Doc.' Alexei slid onto his bunk. 'I've been wanting to ask if you know anything about these. I haven't wanted to pry, so I thought I'd wait until I knew you better.' He pointed to several stains on the underside of the bunk's coverlet.

Bogoraz peered owlishly through his lenses. 'The poor chap was in a bad state before I got him off to hospital,' he said softly. 'He'd been concealing the bleeding for some time. Shouldn't say it to you, Slepak, but your predecessor wasn't up to his job. The Old Man gave him a hell of a time. The tuberculosis didn't help.'

'When we're off duty, Doc,' Alexei interrupted, 'I'm Alexei, if you want it that way. I'm rude enough to call you "Doc", aren't I?' He felt the tension easing between them, but what was Bogoraz trying to tell him at this hour? 'How long have you been in *Uranus*?'

'Since she re-commissioned; I joined with the Old Man.' The doctor's voice dropped. 'It's been bloody awful on my own … Alexei. Grenz's predecessor, Vilms, was useless — just waiting to get out. And Lessner … but perhaps you're already beginning to realize what he's like.'

'Drinks too much. I never know where I am with him,' Alexei said guardedly.

'If *you* don't, chum, how the hell do you think the troops feel?'

'He's afraid of them, underneath the bluster.' Slepak liked the doctor's frank approach — he was sure he could trust him. The relationship between the doctor of a small ship and the number one was always a special one.

'They despise him. One moment he's the martinet, trying to compete with the efficient ships; the next, he's a popularity-jack, allowing the skivers to get away with murder. I'd rate him as a schizophrenic, with his depressions and erratic behaviour. That's why he's been passed over. The near-miss in the Baltic lost him his promotion — that, and our punishment returns. *Uranus* is always top of the pops.'

'What happened in the Baltic?'

A smile transformed Bogoraz's intelligent face. 'There was a fearful balls-up off Kaliningrad during the work-up. I was on the bridge with Lessner, who was conducting a communication exercise. Both diesels broke down during that forenoon, the second engine just as the other squadron was taking up station. We missed *Arcturus* by a couple of metres. Our main bearings had run hot. The tug finally got us alongside and when the chief opened up, he found sand in both boxes.'

'An inquiry?'

'No — the Old Man spoke to the ship's company and tried to hush the whole thing up, insinuating that the Klaipeda yard must have been responsible, after repairs to our emergency generator. We all knew the explanation was phoney, because of what had gone on before.' The doctor was chain-smoking. He half-turned towards Alexei. 'Not boring you? You ought to know what's been going on — if you're to handle what's coming to us.' He kept his voice low; whenever the quartermaster's footsteps padded overhead, his words dropped to a whisper.

'What went on before?' Slepak asked.

'We had been running from Kaliningrad for nearly eighteen months. The troops were well dug in with the locals — some of the older men had their women-folk and families established there. *Uranus* was on to a good thing: regular six-week patrols in the south-western Atlantic approaches, then ten days in harbour. As you probably guessed, the previous commissar was useless, though a malleable, understanding chap: a bottle of vodka worked wonders with him. He had considerable influence with the Old Man; the troops naturally latched on to this bonus. Then the famous signal came through on the day of Yanov's wedding, the youngest of our leading ROs.'

Slepak fetched the glasses from his toilet cupboard. He poured a couple of slugs and pushed the tot across. '*Na zdorovye…!* What signal?'

'Ordering us to join the Black Sea Fleet in Sevastopol. We were to sail at the end of the month — just over three weeks. The news came as a bombshell. The truth is that we had become slack; we were taking too much for granted, though. "Ivan" can't see beyond his nose. The coxswain even saw your predecessor to put forward a request to see the captain privately on behalf of the ship's company. Firstly, to represent the concern of the troops at being so suddenly shifted to the Black Sea Fleet.'

'And what else?'

'He wanted to plead Vize's request to bring his motorbike on board for the passage. The able seaman has relatives in Yalta.'

'What happened?'

'Your predecessor was always afraid of the Old Man. Lessner threw one of his tantrums and refused both requests. And, of course, the details of the sabotage incident soon leaked out — *Uranus* became the squadron joke.'

'How did the troops react?' Alexei asked.

'If Lessner had only listened sympathetically, the ship's morale might not have deteriorated as it has. As the doctor, I tend to know what's going on: things simmered in the messdeck until the atmosphere became very tense. Number one broke down and had to leave the ship. Then came the final incident, two days before sailing.'

'The cutting of the ring main?' Alexei asked. 'Baugersky told me about it.'

The doctor nodded. 'They couldn't hush that one up. The cable was replaced. Commissar Vilms was sacked and Grenz joined two hours before we sailed from Kaliningrad. The inquiry was ordered to be held in Sevastopol. They were all waiting for us when we arrived — no need to tell you that our reputation had preceded us ... but the inquiry proved nothing. We hoped that with a keen commissar and the advent of a new first lieutenant, the ship would come to her senses. That's what the C-in-C was hoping for — a new broom.'

'Are things any better yet?' Alexei was not fishing for compliments, but the doctor sitting before him was a realist.

'To be honest, I think they're worse; perhaps I'm ultra-sensitive and looking for trouble. But while several personalities remain in the ship, I can't see much improvement, unless you and Grenz really crack down ... but our commissar hasn't got much time for you, has he, Alexei?'

'He hates my guts, beneath his suave politeness. We've got to tolerate each other. How would *you* put things right, Nikolai?'

'Find another captain.' Bogoraz had spoken softly, but his eyes had not wavered. 'You'll have to watch your step, Alexei. I'm certain Grenz has informers in the ship — Ordinary Seaman Richter, the officers' steward is one. He looks after you, too, doesn't he?'

'There's something unpleasant about him.'

The doc smiled sadly. 'And what about Grenz?' he asked. 'He's a strange one.'

'A fanatic. The troops are frightened of him. We haven't much choice: do we crack down hard or do we try to bring them round gently?'

Bogoraz sat for a long moment, watching the smoke spiralling to the exhaust vent. Then he said: 'You've *got* to go carefully, Alexei. You mustn't push them much further, in my judgement. And you know another cause for the unrest, don't you? I know you've checked all the troops' papers.'

Alexei met the shrewd eyes regarding him. 'Fomin, the leading seaman?'

Bogoraz nodded. 'Ex-*Storozhevoy*, the mutiny ship. And Able Seaman Salza: dis-rated leading seaman, three years in Siberia.'

'Who knows about these two? Their papers are confidential, except to the commissar, myself and the Old Man.'

'I know that the captain has never got round to it. Too interested in other things — booze and his eternal sing-songs.' Bogoraz shook his head in disgust. 'Lessner's evenings make me want to puke. Grown men, forced to sing dirty ditties until all hours in his cabin … pathetic.'

Alexei grinned. 'Lessner's first sing-song had me wondering what sort of an outfit I had joined. So bloody childish — all I wanted was sleep.'

'He has these sessions at least twice a month. Imagine the troops' reaction — the row keeps them awake in the messdecks.'

'Well, Doc?'

'Watch it, Alexei: you see, I know what's going on.'

CHAPTER TWELVE

After the hectic three weeks' work-up, when all departments were put through their paces by the staff of the Black Sea Fleet's training section, *Uranus* sailed at 0800 on Monday, 23 June, for her final inspection. On board was C-in-C's training staff, a specialist examining officer to each department. Captain Lessner was at his most benevolent when he took his ship to sea, gleaming now in her fresh paint, the bosun's calls shrilling as the ship swept by C-in-C's headquarters, the admiral's flag streaming in the half-gale which was blowing from the south-west.

There was a sea running outside. With a quartering wind, *Uranus* settled on a course parallel to the coast. She headed towards Balaclava, and the exercises began in earnest.

The internal drills were carried out first, in the hope that the weather might ease down by the afternoon for the seamanship evolutions. The communications department, being the *raison d'être* of the ship's existence, bore the brunt. Simulator transmissions from the base, representing the West's radio warfare arsenal, swamped the ether, until CREA Litke was sweating to keep his action team abreast of the work. He was not helped by Perstev's interference, so it was not surprising that eventually someone had to fall right in it — and that it had to be Reek's section. The leading RO had failed to pick up a distinguishing group — one of the junior ROs, Chalidze, had missed it and Reek had taken the brunt.

The captain had been in the office; as soon as he realized what had gone wrong, he lammed into Leading RO Reek, bawling at him from less than a metre's range, in front of the staff officer.

The tirade had been embarrassing (a man would not speak to his dog so contemptuously). Reek maintained a dignified silence. Alexei Slepak had eased through the door for fresh air, disgusted by the exhibition — but he had not missed the hate smouldering in Reek's eyes.

The engine room inspection proceeded throughout the day. The wind eased at noon and the ship turned back to her reciprocal course. When the staff had finished their midday meal, presided over by shifty-eyed Officer Steward Richter, the afternoon's fun and games began: 'Hoist out the kedge anchor on the for'd crane'; 'Fire in engine room'; 'collision abreast port side of bridge — holed below waterline. Rig collision mat.' All had gone reasonably well, until, finally: 'Man overboard, starboard side. Away starboard lifeboat!'

The first lieutenant always lowered the boats at sea, if he was available. Slepak took charge in the break by the funnel. The motor cutter was slipped smoothly and Able Seaman Saha, coxswain by virtue of his seamanlike qualities, picked up the lifebuoy at the first attempt. While the cutter was plunging back alongside in the swell that was still running, the hands prepared the falls for hoisting. The captain had allowed *Uranus*'s bows to fall off, to provide a lee, but the ship was rolling heavily.

Alexei sensed that the commissar was taking an interest behind him on the veranda deck. The buffer (mate of the upper deck) was taking charge at the guard rails and supervising the tending of the wire falls.

This was the moment that mattered, when the boat was wallowing beneath her davits, trying to hook on to the blocks. Salza knew his stuff: as soon as the bowman held up his hand to show that the for'd block was hooked on, Salza struggled with the stern-sheetsman to hook on the after fall. Alexei was watching, concentrating on this vital moment, waiting for the stern-sheetsman to raise his hand. Even then, Slepak would wait for the coxswain's report, '*Hooked on!*'

Uranus was gathering way: the captain had shouted an engine order and was trying to beat the gun, though his number one had not yet reported 'Boat clear of the water.' Slepak waited impatiently, wondering what was holding up the coxswain, when he saw Salza scrambling for'd again to help the bowman. He was shouting and signalling to the buffer to give him more scope in the for'd fall. Slepak placed the hailer to his lips: 'What's the delay, Cox'n?'

As the man glanced upwards in impatience, the for'd block jerked free when the boat fell into the trough. The fall sprang upwards. Slepak heard Salza's warning yell as the cutter instantly swung beam-on, dipping her bows into the sea. In seconds she was half-swamped and almost rolled over; then she was being towed stern-first at several knots from the after fall. Salza had been catapulted into the water and was fighting for his life as the boat pushed him under.

The captain was shouting from the starboard wing at the helmsman. Grenz was bellowing at Slepak, his tirade audible to all the hands in the vicinity. 'Why didn't you hoist right away, you bloody fool?' He was stomping down the ladder to confront Slepak with further abuse.

Alexei ignored him and continued to take charge, while the way came off the ship. They fished Salza from the water, unhooked the after fall and secured the boat on the quarter, sending hands down to bail her out. He relieved the crew and Pyotr Fomin, the upper deck leading hand, brought her to the falls again and hooked on. When the boat was griped-to, Slepak turned to the bridge and reported to the captain. The C-in-C's senior training officer was leaning across the bridge rail, a smirk on his face.

'First motor cutter secured for sea,' Slepak reported. 'I'll be in my cabin, until you want me, sir.' He saw Lessner's embarrassment and the anger in his flushed face. 'I'm not used to being reprimanded by anyone other than you, sir — certainly not in front of the hands.' Slepak walked off the bridge, forcing Grenz to step aside as he made for the bridge ladder.

The sailing signal came through on their way back to base. After picking up mail, watering and fuelling, *Uranus* was to sail at 0800 the next morning to join the Mediterranean Task Force. She was to spend a few days at Mersa Matruh, Libya, on acclimatization trials (she would be fitted with a better type of ventilation during her next refit). She was then to stand-by the NATO exercises which were due shortly.

The captain had sent for Slepak, as soon as he had set course for Sevastopol and could leave the bridge. It had been an awkward meeting. Grenz had stood in the background, silent, missing nothing. Lessner tried to smooth over the incident, but Slepak refused to apologize. The meeting ended abruptly, but all three men knew where they stood.

'I hold myself responsible to you, sir.' Slepak was addressing the captain, but he had turned his head and was staring at Grenz. 'You're the captain. If the commissar wishes to complain about me, I request that he does so in your presence only. Permission to carry on, sir, please?' He turned about and quit the cabin.

The encounter had certainly cleared the air. Grenz masked his feelings and was more wary with the wardroom. Alexei knew he had made a dangerous enemy — unpleasant, when living at close quarters in a small ship.

Uranus secured alongside North Corner at 1700, the staff having declared her as fit to join the fleet; certain recommendations would be forwarded later to her commanding officer.

The remainder of the evening was hectic for them all. Amidst the bustle all around him, Alexei snatched a minute's peace in the seclusion of his cabin to read Katya's letter. It was date-stamped 18 June and had been posted in Leningrad:

My darling, a quick note to tell you the wonderful news: I've got the assistant receptionist's job in Yalta — a little hotel near the Ukraine sanatorium — the Seaview. It's almost too good to be true, isn't it? They want me as soon as I can get down there, but I've got to give in my notice here first. I feel like losing the money and coming straight on down to you. Will write again as soon as I've everything fixed up. I just thought you'd like to know — and I can't resist telling you. Soon to be together again. I love you. Katenka.

That was all.

Alexei snatched a quick bite of supper and went ashore. He got through to her from The Heights Hotel. The phone call cost him a day's pay, but the sound of her voice gave him back his sense of proportion. Katya was reality. Life would be bearable, even in *Uranus*, if they could be together again. 'Write care of Fleet Post Office,' he had said, before ringing off. 'That will always find us.'

The sun was setting behind the hills on the far side of the harbour. A rose afterglow washed the concrete buildings that were the modern city. Alexei began walking back to North Corner. He could just distinguish *Uranus*, the outboard ship of the trot. The 'Blue Peter ', the General Recall, was fluttering at her masthead.

CHAPTER THIRTEEN

Izmir, in Turkish Asia Minor, had suffered a calamitous earthquake. *Uranus* sailed that night to act as 'guard ship' for Russian nationals and to provide assistance if the Turkish authorities requested it. She was to continue to Mersa Matruh as soon as her presence became superfluous in Izmir.

Captain Lessner was the first to sight the pall of smoke against the breaking dawn, shortly after *Uranus* had passed Foça abeam to port. He reduced speed and the ship crawled along the north shore of the bay until she turned into the narrows opening to the stricken city of Izmir. Then they smelt the acrid stench from the earthquake fires. No shipping moved; the port was dead. *Uranus* anchored in the dirty waters half a mile from the harbour, the only foreign warship to have arrived.

The captain sent his commissar ashore in the motor cutter to make contact with the authorities, while Slepak organized the two armed landing-parties. 'The Turks are asking for help in maintaining law and order,' Grenz reported at nine-thirty. 'The town is paralyzed and looting has broken out. They don't know yet the extent of the disaster, how many dead and injured. They're hard pushed organizing rescue parties for those trapped in the buildings.'

Slepak took the first cutter, Marc Klavitter the second. Nine armed sailors, a leading hand and a signalman with a portable radio comprised the landing party in each boat. 'Do what you can,' the captain had ordered. 'Contact our consul — he may need help in protecting our nationals.'

They left the boats with their crews at the landing stage. Slepak and Klavitter marched their men through the docks. The police at the barrier stared at them, unable to comprehend, and waved them through. It was the same story all the way into the city — the populace was numbed by the disastrous earthquake, unable to realize the enormity of the catastrophe. Communications were non-existent, public transport was at a standstill.

Klavitter commandeered a lorry which he found tilted on its side against a smashed telegraph pole. They righted the truck and managed to start the engine. 'Hang on to it, Marc,' Slepak ordered. 'Put a guard on it when we get into the town. We may need it in a hurry.' They squeezed themselves into the rattling vehicle and drove towards the fires still smouldering in what must have been one of the main squares. The route petered out, blocked by the rubble from collapsed buildings. Tall blocks of flats leaned drunkenly; dogs roamed the once-busy thoroughfare. Slepak passed an old crone, dressed in black from head to foot, a dead cat in her arms. She was staring straight ahead and laughing shrilly. They could still hear her, as they began scrambling across the masonry.

They arrived in what presumably had been an important shopping area. Broken glass strewed the streets, shutters flapped from windows, sun-blinds trailed in tatters from smashed shop fronts. Small arms fire rattled from inside a large store on their right.

On the far side of the building the road was barred by a cordon of uniformed militia. The officer-in-charge was a tough-looking brute: he held up his hand and made it plain that the Russian party could advance no further. They exchanged pleasantries in English, swapping cigarettes, but it was obviously useless for the landing parties to try and reach the consulate. The consul could have no idea yet how many Russians had been caught by the earthquake, nor the numbers needing emergency housing or transport back to the Soviet Union. The president had declared a national emergency and the imposition of martial law. The army was in control; terrorists and looters were being shot on sight.

'I've got trouble in this big store,' the Turkish officer explained, waving his automatic towards the six-storied building. Curtains flapped from the smashed windows; through the splintered display panels of the ground floor, half-clothed pink dummies leaned grotesquely. Automatic rifle fire echoed down the street.

'We're waiting for them to come out.' The Turkish officer swung the barrel of his gun carelessly across the entrance. 'The major is inside at the other end; he'll soon winkle them out. He could do with your help, if you'd like to lend a hand. You Russians are good at this sort of thing.' Slepak could still hear his laughter as Klavitter pushed through the revolving doors.

It was dark inside, but on the far side of the ground floor flames were flickering through the billowing smoke.

'Take the first floor, Marc,' Slepak commanded. 'I'll start at the top and work my way down. If you bump into the major, tell him we're clearing the floors for him.'

'Right, Number One, but do we want to be involved? There's no point in risking our blokes just to keep the Turkish officer happy, is there?' His arrogance was infuriating, but Klavitter was right. 'We can't help at the consulate,' he continued in the gloom. 'If we become separated, rendezvous at the boats?'

'Yes. Keep in touch on the radio.'

Klavitter had drawn his pistol. 'Leading Seaman Fomin,' he ordered, 'gather the hands around and follow me.'

'Come on, Buffer,' Slepak called to Petty Officer Vritsky, who was in charge of the first section. 'Don't shoot unless you're forced to. Clear the floors, that's all.'

'Aye, aye, sir.'

Slepak heard the safety catches being released while he quietly led the way up the circular stairway. He was out of breath when he reached the sixth floor. 'Spread out. Meet at the other end.'

He took the middle aisle: the buffer moved out to the right, while the rest of the party spread evenly across the floor. He lifted his hand and, pistol cocked before him as he crouched to the level of the counter, he moved silently forwards.

This was the first time he had been exposed to possible fire. This fear presumably evaporated with habit. Why was it that the soldiers he had known seemed to have acquired a contempt for flying bullets? He crouched lower, his instincts entirely different. He had no wish to lose his life here, cut to pieces by trigger-happy looters. Katenka would never forgive him. He smiled in the darkness, as he reached for the far end of the floor.

'No one here, sir,' the buffer was calling.

'Okay. All present?'

'Istomin's missing, sir,' one of the seamen called in the darkness. 'He was on my left.'

'Tell him to shake it up.' Slepak moved towards the end doorway marked 'Emergency Exit'.

'He's here, sir,' the buffer called, and then he gave Istomin the rough edge of his repertoire. Slepak and the buffer were achieving that easy relationship which often exists in a small ship between first lieutenant and chief bosun's mate.

'Okay, Buffer, we'll clear the next floor.'

They descended to the fifth and repeated the process, crouching behind the counters which were laden with electronic goods — radios, record players, TVs, cameras, typewriters, the lot. As they were reaching the far side, Slepak heard shooting from the floor below. He felt his heart pumping against his ribs.

'All here, Buffer? Stand by — we'll rush the next floor if we have to.'

'Sorry, sir, but Istomin's adrift again — and where's Zubov?' The buffer was working himself up. 'Bloody skivers,' he growled. 'Where the flaming hell've you been? What you got there, Istomin?' There was a crash and a muffled curse. Slepak moved across impatiently.

Istomin, a small man, had slung his gun; his pockets bulged and from his other shoulder a camera dangled in its case. Zubov stood sheepishly behind him, a tape-recorder slung across his back, a radio and a calculator clutched in his free hand. He was older than Istomin and a candidate for leading hand.

'Put it all back,' Slepak snapped. 'I'll see you when we get back on board. You're a bloody disgrace.'

'Hurry,' Vritsky snarled at them. 'You useless shower, you're holding us up.' He turned to Slepak. 'Sorry, sir.'

'You deal with them, Buffer. Make sure there's no more of this.' He moved slowly towards the stairway. 'Ready?'

They tiptoed the last few steps. Slepak waited until the sailors were close behind him. He crept forwards, signalling them to spread out again. He flattened himself on the floor as a hail of bullets splattered the wall.

The buffer opened fire to his right, the flame spitting from the barrel of his automatic. The floor echoed with the rattle of shots, debris flew about them, there was a shout from the far end. Alexei glimpsed a silhouette across the stairway exit. He levelled his pistol and fired.

'*Rush 'em!*'

He heard his men about him, stampeding down the aisles, cursing and shouting encouragement to each other. He halted them at the exit doors, then cautiously crept down the circular stairway. He stepped across a slumped body, which the buffer prodded with his boot. He slipped down to the third floor — he was not going to be caught a second time. He slithered prone as soon as he felt his team behind him. A dark figure loomed from the corner and Alexei was gazing into the barrel of an automatic weapon.

'Major Kessan,' a large Turkish man muttered in a broken American accent. 'You're the Russians?'

Slepak stood up and the man took his hand. 'We caught 'em as they came down,' the soldier said. 'If there're any left alive, they'll not get far. The store's surrounded.'

'There's another of my party on the first floor,' Slepak told him. 'The looters will have to get past them.'

The Turkish man shook his head. 'I sent them away... They weren't very helpful.' He paused a moment, then added apologetically, 'My men aren't so careful, once they start shooting. I didn't want your chaps caught in the crossfire.'

There was a staccato volley from somewhere outside the building; a scream, then silence.

'We can go now,' the Turkish man said. 'My compliments to your captain; tell him we're glad you've arrived.'

'Come on board when you can, Major. You'll be welcome.'

They shook hands and, once outside, Slepak tried to contact Klavitter on the radio. 'I can't raise them, sir,' the signalman reported.

'Back to the ship, Buffer. We can't do much more here.'

They found the truck, but there was no message from Klavitter's section. When Slepak reached the landing stage, he was surprised to find only the first cutter. Able Seaman Salza was waiting with the engine running. He saluted as he approached Slepak.

'Lieutenant Klavitter's compliments, sir: he's returned to the ship. MEM Rykov was hit, and they've taken him back to sick bay.'

CHAPTER FOURTEEN

The heat haze shimmered about *Uranus* where she lay swinging to her cable in the blistering heat of noon. She was a smarter ship, Slepak thought, than when he had first seen her. Her side was clean; the translucent colours of the sea undulated in gentle motion across the white upperworks gleaming in the midday sunlight.

This earthquake emergency had helped to pull the ship together. Since the panic started in Sevastopol, on the evening of the twenty-sixth, the ship had taken on a new sense of purpose. This forenoon's excitement had forced the troops in the landing parties to stop and think: the horrors in the aftermath of the earthquake and the misery of the population had sobered up the hotheads. Grievances magnified themselves out of proportion when men were cooped up in a small ship during the heat of a Mediterranean summer.

As Able Seaman Salza brought his boat across the ship's stern, Slepak was surprised to see that the second motorboat had been hoisted.

'Thank you, Cox'n.' He nipped up the gangway and hurried for'd to report to Lessner.

'I'll talk to the commissar about the situation,' the captain concluded. 'Unless the authorities have brought things under control, there's not much I can do. You've told them to contact us if they need help?'

'Yes, sir. They're trying to get through to our consul.' Slepak hesitated, then added, 'When would you like to see Zubov and Istomin? I think I should pass them on to you, sir.'

'If the Turkish officers had found out about the looting, it wouldn't have reflected well on us, would it?' Lessner's face clouded as he drummed his fingers on the desk. 'Bring them up at once.'

Lessner had overreacted when dealing with the two seamen. He awarded each seven days' cells, locked in the two cabooses which were without daylight or proper ventilation in the fo'c'sle head. He stopped all leave and cancelled contact with the shore, even to the postman's run; and he cancelled the Wednesday make-and-mend — 'to make 'em realize that anyone who brings discredit on my ship will bloody well catch it hot and strong.' And, turning on his heel from the defaulters' table, he retired to his cabin.

Alexei Slepak felt the tense atmosphere as he entered the wardroom for lunch. Klavitter was talking more loudly than usual, pontificating upon the virtues of the long 'N' course with the electrical officer, Baugersky, who glanced up uneasily at the first lieutenant as he entered. The subject — probably Slepak's decision to take the two seamen to the captain for punishment — had obviously been rapidly changed.

During the afternoon, Slepak made it his business to be seen about the upper deck: the buffer had unreeled the 10cm hoist-wire of the crane in order to grease it. Slepak had taken the opportunity to check the last test date.

'Yes, Cox'n?' He turned as the coxswain came up behind him.

He had little confidence in this hatchet-faced little man. At forty-one, the oldest rating in the ship, Stefan Korolev looked older. He was not firm enough with the hands, preferring to be all things to all men. He was a scraggy specimen but was no fool; his eyes were too close together, and Alexei was never sure if he told the truth. The ship's company were too familiar with him — perhaps Korolev's close working with the easy-going Vilms, the departed commissar, had undermined the coxswain's authority.

'We're getting low on fresh vegetables, sir. Can I send Dusty ashore to see if he can win some off the locals?'

'Sorry, 'Swain. No one's to go ashore until further orders. Break into the frozen foods.'

'Stocks are low on them too, sir. Didn't have time, with our pier-head jump, to restock.' Korolev lowered his voice: 'No good asking the captain again, sir? It's hot in the messdeck. We could do with lettuces and fresh fruit.'

'You heard what I said, Cox'n.'

'Yes, sir. Aye, aye, sir.' Korolev saluted and clambered slowly down the after ladder.

The day wore on, the hands trying to keep to the shade. They worked half-heartedly, and Alexei was forced to send for the buffer.

'For God's sake, Buffer, what's got into 'em? A lot of old women.'

'They don't appreciate having their make-and-mend cancelled, sir,' Vritsky said softly. 'Sea watches last night, sir. The middle-watchmen are chokka.'

'They'd better buck up their ideas. It's your job to chase 'em, Buffer — but I've news for you: the captain's just told me he may be landing all hands tomorrow.'

'Yes, sir?' Vritsky glanced at him. 'More police duties?'

'Burial parties. If the locals can't cope with the dead, they'll be asking for our help.'

The first lieutenant had no chance for a few days to go round the ship again. He spent Thursday contacting the city authorities, who were at last sorting themselves out. The casualties had been worse than feared and the bulldozers had not arrived. Pick-and-shovel was the only method of disposing of the corpses in this heat. A tented village was being organized outside the city, but until the encampment was ready, the mainland troops were not being flown in.

On the third day, Alexei went ashore again to inspect his landing parties. Theirs was a disgusting task: the stench, in spite of the muslin masks with which they had been issued, was nauseating. The heat was bad enough, but the flies made even the older men blanch. When Slepak carried out rounds himself on Saturday night, the silence as he threaded his way between the four messes was more eloquent than words.

He had decided to ask the Old Man for permission to give a lie-in on the Sunday morning — the men needed it after the appalling week. Lessner had glared at him and told him not to be soft with the hands, but before lunch on that Sunday morning he was again exuding charm and smiles. The pre-lunch drinking continued until well past one-thirty; Slepak did not miss the contempt lurking in the steward's eyes when they sat down to eat.

His cabin was unbearable during the afternoon, with the ship lying at anchor. *Uranus* might have been a ghost-ship: the hands had their heads down, stretched out on the upper deck and following the shade round as the ship swung. The officers' preserve was on the veranda deck surrounding the funnel. The wardroom was sleeping off the effects of lunch; Slepak had settled his camp bed along the edge of the veranda, hoping to catch any up-draught. He was dozing off when he noticed an untidy reel-cover lashed abaft the engine intakes; it was spoiling the 'squared-off' appearance of the area, which had been free of loose gear. When he woke he would check up on it.

'You sent for me, Number One?'

Klavitter was propping himself in the doorway of the first lieutenant's cabin, the cigarette smoke curling from between his fingers.

'I found a motorbike covered up on the boat deck. The buffer tells me it's yours.'

The navigator's bushy eyebrows rose. 'Didn't you know, then, Number One? Oh, I'm sorry... You weren't on board. I bumped into the commissar. He said he thought it would be all right to stow it, provided the ship could use it when required.' Klavitter gazed through the scuttle, the corners of his mouth twitching. His heavy, red face, his insolent eyes, his arrogance were anathema to Alexei.

'Does the captain know about it?'

'Haven't asked him. I thought Grenz was good enough.'

Alexei rose from his chair and faced Klavitter. 'You're a fool, Pilot — and not very honest. You've gone over my head and I don't like it one bit.' He jabbed a finger in Klavitter's chest. 'Your action explains a lot — you're deliberately making things difficult for me.'

'Why should I want to do that?'

'God knows. We're trying to make something of this ship and you go and do something bloody silly. It's serious enough that you looted the machine — couldn't your little head remember that the captain turned down Able Seaman Vize's request in Kaliningrad? He wasn't allowed to ship his bike down to Sevastopol.'

'The looters would have burnt the store down,' Klavitter retorted. 'What was the point of watching valuable stuff going up in smoke? Grenz and the others didn't take it the way you have.' He flicked his cigarette ash onto the deck.

Slepak forced his way past Klavitter and slammed his cabin door. 'Shut up and listen to me, Lieutenant Klavitter. I am now officially warning you that I find your attitude objectionable. I have been dissatisfied with your attitude ever since I joined the ship. If you don't buck up and put your personal feelings behind you — as from NOW — I shall ask the captain to have you relieved. Is that clear?'

'Is that all, sir?'

'Clear out. I shan't warn you again.'

Slepak felt better as soon as the man had quit. But the reprimand was too late — the atmosphere in the ship was already explosive. The motorcycle incident could only make things worse: each time a man passed that yellow Honda beneath its canvas cover, he would feel incensed by the injustice. To clear his own yard-arm, Slepak must raise the matter with the Old Man. The troublemakers would latch on to this — every man on board was poised on the lip of a smouldering volcano.

And that night the anonymous cartoon was found by the coxswain on the ship's company noticeboard.

CHAPTER FIFTEEN

Uranus weighed during the forenoon after the noticeboard affair. Neither the first lieutenant nor the commissar could deal with the matter at once, and neither was sure how best to take it.

During the passage to Egypt, Grenz had deigned to visit Alexei in his cabin. The commissar was positively friendly, as Alexei tried to assess the complex character sitting in front of him.

'I thought we were getting on top of things, Slepak. We've both made mistakes, but we're aiming at the same result. Have you any idea who's behind the unrest?' The grey-green eyes clouded over. Grenz had the dead stare of the cobras that Katenka and Alexei had watched with loathing in the reptile house of the zoo at Kadriorg.

'No idea, Commissar. I've inherited an unhappy ship. What makes her so, you must judge. But you have your own methods of finding out what's going on — it's your job, isn't it?'

Grenz smiled blandly. 'They open up to me sometimes. I encourage them to talk to me in my cabin — difficult, though, this lot.'

'You can't blame them — the navigator's motorbike doesn't help; it was straightforward looting, a bloody sight worse than the paltry lifting for which Zubov and Istomin were hammered. You can't entirely blame the troops, particularly after Vize was refused permission to ship his bike down here.'

'I don't agree with you, Slepak. The Honda can be of use to the ship. It wasn't as if there was any further looting in the navigator's landing party.' Grenz glanced through the scuttle at the blue sea sliding past. 'And the cartoon's appalling — a direct challenge.'

'And bloody funny — under the circumstances.'

'You find it amusing?'

'The artist's a genius — you can identify all of us.' In his mind he could see the cartoon: the pigsty where the porkers snuffled in their own filth, fighting for their food. The stripes of rank on their stubby legs — the likenesses of Lessner, Perstev and Grenz were particularly successful, with their piggy eyes and snouts — and, in the background, a 'Klavitter' pig, astride a yellow Honda propped against the trough. 'I thought the title a bit crude — they might have used something less obvious.'

'"Pigs in Shit" — not very funny. You don't find the thing disgraceful?'

'I think we've asked for it.'

'What are *you* going to do about it?' Grenz asked softly, his eyes meeting Slepak's.

'The captain's got to clear lower deck and talk to them. Matruh is his first opportunity.'

Captain Lessner addressed his ship's company at 0900 on Friday, 25 July. The plating of the welldeck was already hot underfoot when the company assembled in two ranks with their backs to the crane pedestal, in a half-circle around him.

Grenz stood behind him on his left, Slepak on his other side, the remainder of the officers in a phalanx behind the trio. The muscles behind Lessner's knee were trembling and shaking the twill of his trousers. Slepak glanced at the flushed, tanned face nervously trying to impress the younger men before him. The captain began quietly, systematically reviewing the events of the past weeks.

Alexei was watching the ship's company, and particularly the older men: the coxswain, Korolev, on one side, gazing across the harbour of Mersa Matruh; beside him was Chief Marine Engineering Artificer Barabsky and, separated from them both, Chief Radio Electrical Artificer Mikhail Litke. Korolev and Barabsky looked away as they met Slepak's gaze; Litke, a large man, pale-faced from the artificial lighting in the monitoring offices, held Slepak's glance. Was that mockery lurking in those dark eyes? Or was he signalling his loyalty to his boss, the first lieutenant and head of his department? Or was he, an intelligent senior rating, trying to indicate to Slepak that being lectured by such a captain in such circumstances was both ludicrous and humiliating? It was Slepak who had to shift his gaze.

The younger hands stood sullenly 'at ease', caps behind their backs. The majority looked straight ahead, but Istomin was fidgeting, his head jerking from side to side. Zubov was just visible in the rear rank, but his massive face was expressionless.

The leading hands stood at either end of the ranks, Leading Seaman Pyotr Fomin next to the end man, Able Seaman Solomon Salza. Those two were giving nothing away: Fomin, the oldest leading hand, thirty-one and an ex-petty officer (he had been disrated after the *Storozhevoy* affair), medium height, fair-haired, uniform always neatly pressed, was a difficult man to fathom. His subtle and derisory contempt for authority appealed to his impressionable and younger messmates but, Alexei guessed, his sardonic attitude failed to compensate for the bitterness that Fomin felt for the injustices of life's batterings.

And Salza, Fomin's chum, both drawn together by age and the knowledge that they were the only real seamen in the ship — what was he thinking? Solomon Salza had proved his stubbornness already. His Siberian experiences had forged him into what he was: short, sturdy, tough, obstinate, with immense self-control. Reek, the leading radio operator, tall and rangy, hatchet-faced, was standing alongside his 'oppo', leading RO Yanov, the younger man at twenty-three, wanting to get on. The third leading RO, Lange, was on duty in the monitoring room, the only man excused from today's 'clear lower deck'.

The engine room department lined the port side, a quiet, pale lot, with the senior leading marine engineering mechanic, Nakhimov, alongside the other two leading MEMs. Nakhimov was black-bearded, a rollicking type, brimming over with humour, permanently in his scruffy, oil-streaked overalls; when a sing-song took place in the messdeck, he would be leading it with his concertina and his splendid bass voice.

Were the troops aware of Lessner's nervousness? Slepak was sure that Litke had not missed this evidence of weakness; he *might* keep the knowledge to himself — he could never be certain with Litke, a mysterious, aloof man.

The captain had recited the Acts of War, the bible giving teeth to naval discipline, and an hour had passed. The men were restless, bored and conspicuously unimpressed by the captain's implied threats. Lessner nodded to his first lieutenant.

'Ship's Company ... *'sshun!*' Slepak saluted as the captain left the silent welldeck.

'Fall out the officers.'

They turned and saluted him. He faced the hands.

'Turn right, *dis-miss!*'

One advantage derived from working out of the hellhole that was Mersa Matruh in midsummer: the air-conditioning trials were carried out under realistic conditions. After eleven weeks of shadowing NATO's Mediterranean fleets, the ten-day refit which had been booked for *Uranus* at Valetta, to install the air-conditioning plant, would come as a break for everyone on board. Captain Lessner, three weeks after the non-event when he had addressed his ship's company, had the sense to inform them of the future programme. Living on board would be impossible, so accommodation had been arranged for officers and men in the submarine depot ship, *Tobol.* The Malta refit would take place from 17 to 29 October and four days' night-leave would be granted to each watch.

The ship had seemed to settle down at Matruh, in spite of the heat. Limited shore leave contributed to the apparent calm and, when *Uranus* sailed for the first time to shadow the Americans and Italians exercising off Pantellaria, Slepak felt that at last the ship's company was finding stability. One evening, while taking the air with the doc on the upper deck, Alexei listened to Bogoraz's fresh warning not to be misled by the apparent tranquillity. Slepak had remonstrated with him. 'You're becoming like some of your patients, Doc — too sensitive. You're looking for trouble.'

Uranus stood off at three miles from the Americans: it was fascinating watching those Western warships, the gigantic carriers creaming through the blue of the Mediterranean, their destroyer escorts trying to keep up; the far-flung frigate screens and — invisible, but lurking in the depths of these middle seas — the hunter-killer submarines. And, like albatrosses, the warships of his own navy were shadowing the Western ships, sometimes dangerously so. To Alexei Slepak, it had all seemed a childish waste of time and money, these naval war games, a criminal waste of the world's resources while the developing nations starved. Both sides knew that the whole thing was a hollow bluff: neither Russia nor America would ever press the button; the risk to the planet came from the minor powers, now holding in their hands dangerous toys with which to blackmail the planet. Brezhnev's chickens had come home to roost.

After exercises, *Uranus* was ordered to work between the islands of Linosa and Lampedusa for a couple of days before returning to bunker at Hammamet. She was to operate from this Tunisian harbour, anchored outside the three-mile limit, until the refit. It was here that the cancer began to spread again through the life of the ship.

The erratic mails were a major cause in the deterioration of morale, Slepak was convinced. After being lost in the central Mediterranean, with only the sight of an occasional bulk-carrier or container-ship moving along the horizon to break the monotony, it was depressing to return to the anchorage only to discover that the mail had been diverted to Matruh. Over two months had elapsed before they received their first sack of mail. There had been three letters from Katya, the last in answer to Alexei's announcement of their forthcoming refit in Valetta:

I've cancelled my Yalta job. Now that you've left, I'm glad I have, because I can be a freer agent. Mum and Dad have given me the money for a holiday. I've got a surprise for you, my darling... Dad's application for a visa to Israel is being reconsidered. He decided to test their sincerity and booked three tickets on a charter trip to Malta — one of Intourist's latest gimmicks. THEY'RE LETTING HIM GO! So we're coming to Malta, to be there when you arrive in Uranus *on 17 October... We fly back on the twenty-fourth.*

Alexei sat alone in his cabin, a stupid grin on his face, until Richter knocked on the door to ask whether he was coming to supper. It had been difficult settling down to work afterwards, but eventually he had reached into the drawer for his typewriter — he liked to type his daily orders, as practice, perhaps, for the future.

The drawer was empty. He never lent the machine — he sat motionless, staring through the scuttle. Then he picked up his internal phone. 'Quartermaster, give the coxswain my compliments. Ask him to come and see me,' he ordered.

Korolev had known nothing about it, nor whom to approach when he had been poking about the messdecks asking questions and looking for the machine. The typewriter had returned to Alexei's cabin as mysteriously as it had disappeared — on the next day. Though he had kept the affair quiet — he had decided to inform neither Grenz nor the captain — the incident deeply disturbed Slepak: for the first time, the troublemakers were attacking him personally.

His self-confidence was undermined, he knew that. When he passed the hands on the upper deck or in the passages, he sensed their amusement. The averted eye, the faint smirk was impossible to counter. He felt as if he were treading on quicksand. But mercifully there remained only two more patrols, the next off Sardinia and the last, thirty miles north of Bone.

He was to share the leave-period with Grenz, who was to take second turn. The commissar had been lying low. His relationship with Richter was certainly strange: the steward was too often tapping upon the commissar's cabin door, with the inevitable result — Richter was now shunned by the remainder of the troops. The messdeck buzzed with hints that the spanking new stereo in Grenz's cabin had been picked up ashore, when Richter had gone with Klavitter's landing party. The gear had certainly not been installed when the ship had left Sevastopol — but no one dared accuse the commissar.

Alexei now dealt with Grenz as little as possible: he kept to himself all his suspicions on the troublemakers. He had even laid an elementary trap. He told Richter one day, as the steward was making up the bunk, that he, the first lieutenant, was recommending that Richter should be re-drafted back to the Baltic Fleet as he had originally wanted. At lunchtime on the same day, Grenz had raised the subject of Richter's transfer.

Slepak was beginning to hate this ship. *Uranus* ... the name itself was hostile — a dead planet. *Uranus* ... this unhappy ship, divided against herself. He was sure, in spite of the coxswain's negative attitude and the buffer's obvious reluctance to be sucked into the maelstrom, that Fomin, the ex-PO, was at the root of the unrest. The fact that the leading seaman had been in the crack destroyer, *Storozhevoy*, when she had mutinied in the Baltic, was enough to contaminate him, particularly after being dis-rated. Everyone in *Storozhevoy* at the time of the mutiny, with the KGB's enquiries completed, had seen her ship's company dispersed throughout the fleets. But that had been some time ago, back in '75.

And the ex-camp prisoner, Salza, a fine able seaman, yet refusing to go through for leading hand, what was he up to? At twenty-nine, he was two years younger than his friend, Fomin.

The doc had told Alexei that the communications department, Slepak's own baby, kept itself very much to itself. The ROs were certainly a close lot — Chief REA Litke was a strong character: he ran the department well and never had trouble with his own people. He seemed to have more influence on the ship than either the coxswain or the chief

MEA, who was worn out by his diesels and their appalling noise.

On three occasions, Slepak had tried confidentially to convince the Old Man that the troublemakers must be identified and somehow drafted out of the ship, however difficult it was these days to be rid of them. This surgical operation was easier in a fleet than in a ship on detached duty, but Lessner had shrugged him off: hard work would bring the men to their senses; and the Malta leave would provide other distractions. In a few days, this last patrol would be ended and *Uranus* would be steering for Malta. Alexei had made up his mind to ask Katya to marry him during their next long leave, whether the Lazarevs would be emigrating or not. Whatever her parents' future, or however his relationship with Katya affected his service career, they would share their lives until the end of time.

Four-thirty in the morning and not a touch of dawn from the eastern horizon; still dark and only the caress of the wavelets upon the rocks of St Julian's Bay to disturb this last, precious hour. Alexei would have to leave by six at the latest, to be on time for 'hands fall in' in the Valetta dockyard. An hour and a half of loving and then ... and he committed the future to the furthest recesses of his mind. He turned and encircled Katya's body in the crook of his arm.

'Katenka.'

She sighed and entwined herself about him. And as she slowly awoke to his caresses, his mind retraced the heaven that these past four days had been.

Her parents and she had touched down in the Intourist plane at Luqa last week. Their few days before *Uranus*'s arrival had given them a chance to find the modest room in this comfortable little hotel, The Manoel, which was tucked into the northern curve of St Julian's Bay. Katya had remained with her parents in The Mersetto, the hotel booked by Intourist for this holiday-tour, until 17 October, when she had moved to The Manoel to wait for Alexei.

'Come…' she was whispering in the darkness. She moaned with pleasure as they found each other for the last time. The murmur of the restless sea on the rocks outside their window was the only accompaniment to their lovemaking. They were perfectly attuned, the complement of each other. During these past four days and nights, they had reached heights of happiness which neither knew could exist this side of heaven; the frenzy of their passion beneath the stars by the banks of the Pirita had undergone a subtle change. That Alexei could realize with certainty his sole desire — to give her pleasure as well as to gratify his own — had matured his lovemaking. He had found the control and the peace for which he had craved for so long. And now, in the delirium of these last moments together, Katya was showering him with all the passion of which she was capable.

Afterwards, listening to the waves, she slept for a few minutes, her oval face pale and serene beneath him.

'Katenka, take care. I shan't come to the airport. Keep writing, won't you?'

'When will you be back?'

'After the NATO exercises at the end of November. Sevastopol for Christmas.'

'Shall I try again for that job?'

And so they laid their plans once again; though the future was uncertain, their love for each other was the rock upon which they would build their lives. They would marry as soon as Alexei had finished with *Uranus* and was sent on his 'long course'.

'You'll tell me if your dad gets his visa?' he whispered. 'Allowing him this holiday is a good sign. Go to Israel with them. You're not to wait for me.'

Katya's hands clasped his head and she pulled him down to her, kissing him again and again.

CHAPTER SIXTEEN

Uranus turned to the westward as soon as she had cleared Valetta harbour on the evening of 1 November. She sailed three days late because of electrical problems caused by the new air-conditioning machinery. The main generator had become overloaded, so the yard had fitted an auxiliary diesel in the shelter on the port side of the upper deck, abaft the funnel.

Alexei Slepak had remained on the upper deck to watch the coast slipping past: he recognized the cove of St Julian's, glimpsed momentarily the upper storey of The Manoel, and then the shadows began to slant horizontally across the island. St Paul's Bay opened up briefly; he was just able to identify the islet, white breakers dashing upon the rocks at its base, upon which the Apostle was cast nearly 2,000 years ago. The last rays from the dying sun brushed the base of the night clouds, and the carmine reflection was caressing the soft sandstone buildings of the villages. The little island of Gozo merged into the dark purple horizon, then vanished — and the dream had passed.

Slepak was glad of the workload which followed during the next few weeks. On 2 November, *Uranus* anchored again off Hammamet to pick up mail — the anticipation may have been one reason why there had been no leave-breakers in Malta. Lessner and Grenz also had evidently decided to work more closely together, because the ship soon settled down to the monotony of dogging the Western fleets.

The first patrol from Hammamet lasted until 28 November, a hard time for Litke's team in particular, because the NATO traffic had increased considerably. Why couldn't the 'Enemy' obligingly include the Russian C-in-C in their addresses? The unselfishness would save so much of this interminable processing. How would historians judge this ludicrous farce? The Soviet Mediterranean Task Force was standing-by to shadow the winter Western exercises; the NATO fleet was predicted to be passing through the Straits of Gibraltar on 7 December.

Uranus refuelled at Algiers on 29 November, sailing the next day. 'The Rock' showed through the haze of dawn on the first, where a reconnaissance aircraft of the RAF circled them. Apart from recording the traffic making the passage of the Straits, *Uranus*'s orders were to proceed direct to Madeira for topping up with diesel and fresh provisions at Funchal. She secured to head and stern buoys at midday on 3 December, but, because of the swell, the oiler could not berth alongside until the next morning.

During the forenoon of the fourth, Alexei was in the monitoring room watching Litke training the operators in the new procedures, when the quartermaster appeared to summon the first lieutenant to the captain's cabin. The Old Man had been drinking: his cheeks were flushed, so Slepak waited for the outburst. Lessner thrust the signal towards him: 'The commissar has seen it. The chief's only halfway with his fuelling. Have you anyone ashore, Number One?'

'Yes, sir: the coxswain and the storeman — fresh provisions.' Slepak glanced at the secret signal: the NATO Mediterranean Fleet had sailed two days earlier than predicted. It would be passing through the Straits of Gibraltar during the night of the fifth. The fleet was expected to be steering north-west; *Uranus* was to close and was to be in position during the early hours of 6 December.

'The navigator tells me I've eight hours in hand at maximum cruising speed. Hoist the recall and sound-off on the whistle — that might wake up the coxswain. I'll sail at once.'

'While we're preparing for sea, sir, I'll send the boat in for them.'

'You heard what I said, First Lieutenant. Single-up and stand-by to slip the oiler. Let go the bridle and reeve slip-ropes.'

'Aye, aye, sir.' Alexei was thankful to quit the cabin. He found the chief bosun's mate by the funnel: 'Both watches, Buffer. Special sea-dutymen. Put the buoy-jumper on the buoy, then hoist the motor cutter.'

Eighteen minutes later, Slepak reported that he was ready for sea. Lessner was waiting impatiently on the bridge.

'Coxswain and storeman still ashore, sir.'

'Very good. Ring on main engines. Let go aft.'

Alexei stood in the starboard wing to watch the stern wire being hauled in. The bridge team was going about its business behind him, and then he realized that the Old Man was shouting engine orders. Alexei watched the swirl aft, as both propellers went astern.

'*Wire's not yet clear of the water, sir!*' he shouted.

The inevitable was happening: the signalman aft was jerking up his red flag.

'Starboard propeller's fouled, sir,' he reported. The swirl subsided. The captain stood fuming beside him.

'For God's sake, First Lieutenant! What are those bloody fools doing down there?'

The miserable day dragged on: a seaman skin-diver was sent down to report on the foul-up; the wire was wrapped firmly round the prop. Manual turning of the shaft in the reverse direction failed to unravel the mess. The clearance was beyond ship's staff. Time was lost organizing through sleepy agents the services of a salvage firm and of a working diver, but they could not be on the job until early the next morning. The atmosphere at dinner that night was tense.

At eight the next morning, the ancient diving boat arrived alongside with its red-bonneted diver. He took two hours to cut the wire adrift. It was 10.13 on 5 December when *Uranus* finally cleared the harbour.

Lieutenant Maxim Melvedev, Chief Engineer, always kept clear of the bridge as much as he could. Alexei, who was at the chart table working out the watches with Klavitter, was surprised to see the lean, overalled figure of the engineering officer.

'Where's the captain, Number One?'

'In his cabin, Chief.' Melvedev shrugged his shoulders.

'Vibration in the starboard shaft,' he said. 'I'll have to cut down the revs. Will you tell him, or shall I?'

They both smiled. 'Okay.' The sardonic engineer whom Slepak had begun to respect dropped down the bridge ladder. Five minutes later, the starboard engine was knocked back; the ship was now making good only 12.8 knots.

They missed the NATO force by three and a half hours. Lessner hung on as long as he dared, but finally Litke had reported that they were wasting their time in the monitoring room. The chief REA waited for the captain to compose the signal reporting *Uranus*'s failure. C-in-C would require an explanation on return to Sevastopol, though the wording in Lessner's signal was devious enough perhaps to hoodwink the staff.

Ten minutes later, the signal had been cleared. The irony of it all, Slepak realized later, was that the outgoing signal was passed only a few minutes before the incoming bombshell. If

Lessner could have delayed it only another few minutes, Sevastopol need never have known of his failure. Alexei had come up to the bridge. In Litke's hand was the incoming operational signal, a copy for both captain and commissar.

Jumping from his chair, the captain beckoned Grenz out to the port wing. Slepak watched them, Lessner waving his arms, Grenz coolly appraising, waiting for the storm to subside. Slepak shrugged his shoulders and left the bridge: he would be told later. The buzz would be around the ship already. He was always the last to know.

CHAPTER SEVENTEEN

The only man on board *Uranus* on that morning of Tuesday, 6 December who seemed to relish the new sailing orders was the commissar. When he deigned to lunch that day in the wardroom ('to make a break in his sea-going routine'), he was condescendingly paternal. 'Bissau is the key to our political influence in western Africa,' he announced. 'We must deal with the situation before it gets out of hand.'

He lectured them on the importance of their new mission. Tribal warfare, spilling over from the Fouta Djallon mountains in Guinea, was threatening the stability of the People's Republic in what had once been Portuguese Guinea. The incumbent president had asked for Soviet support. It was hoped that the presence of a Soviet naval vessel and the presence of smart landing parties ashore might calm the situation.

Uranus was to report 'on site' conditions and, if her commissar deemed it necessary, further reinforcements would be despatched. Admiralty was reluctant to do so until the situation really demanded a force with teeth — the African Squadron was busy enough backing up the Cubans and the mercenaries pouring into Djibouti, Dar es Salaam, Mozambique and Beira.

'So we've got a job to do,' Grenz said. 'I hope we'll pull ourselves together. The sooner we've topped up at Funchal and are on our way south to Bissau, the happier we'll be.' Grenz was living in cuckoo-land. Insensitive as he was, he must surely have sensed the reaction of the ship's company?

Slepak had quietly left the table. In the privacy of his cabin, he tried to analyse his reaction to this last turn of the wheel: for himself, he supposed that this departure to the tropics could not affect him much. Where he served was unimportant, provided he could put this job behind him. It was fortunate that they had been issued with tropical gear and that the air-conditioning had been fitted. The fuelling barge had been ordered for 0800, Friday, 9 December. Perhaps the Old Man would be more prudent this time? The ship must be a laughing-stock in Funchal — and sailors, particularly Soviet seamen, did not respond kindly to ridicule. If he wrote to Katya tonight, perhaps he might be able to despatch a mail from Funchal, if the officers could censor the letters in time. Alexei fetched his cap from behind the door. He would find the coxswain and organize a mail — that should cheer up the troops.

They made landfall on Madeira at dawn on 9 December. The cloud hovering over the beautiful island was visible at long range, but *Uranus* was on time for her fuel barge. Lessner agreed to land a mail, because the boat could be hoisted before the chief had finished fuelling. Slepak was working on his correspondence in his cabin — one bonus was the sight of Katya's handwriting.

Trying to hold this ship together was becoming a strain; and, though the foray into West Africa would be hot and unpleasant, the ship's company would be seeing a new world, new cultures — providing Grenz and the Old Man allowed shore leave. It was a pity that circumstances could not have been different.

He wished his Russia did not have such grandiose ideas of political domination. Soviet imperialism applied force through foreign mercenaries and by supplying modern, lethal weapons to other nations. Slepak felt there was something unclean about his country's hypocritical methods.

The doc felt the same about things. The world's rising generation of young men and women, even in the Soviet Union, who enjoyed the privilege of having to do the fighting, were sick of this cynical, filthy business of killing. The Americans had learnt their lesson in Vietnam. Soviet youth, he was sure, would soon be demanding an account of its rulers for their ruthless aggression and exploitation of people. Those in the developing nations, too, would eventually turn on their imperialist masters of the Third Millennium, when they realized that they had lost even the right of free speech.

Alexei picked up the seven-page form for his 'Provisions Return'. What a bloody world this was! 'Love thy neighbour,' the Christians preached. Their message certainly crossed the frontiers, but where were the leaders to put the ideal into practice? He looked up as the electrical officer pushed through the curtains.

'Mind if I shut the door?'

'Go ahead. What's troubling you, Georgiy?'

Baugersky wearily took off his cap and sat on the edge of the bunk. Alexei raised his eyebrows, dreading further sinister news. Georgiy had obstinately retained the red beard he had grown after leaving Leningrad; his humorous blue eyes were clouded with worry.

'I've been checking the maintenance on the air-conditioning plant,' he said, lowering his voice. 'It's buggered.' He held Slepak's eye as the significance of the disaster sunk through.

'The auxiliary diesel?' Slepak asked.

Baugersky shook his head. 'The electric motors. The armatures are burnt out.'

'Both of 'em?'

Georgiy nodded. 'Someone has laid a screwdriver across the commutators.'

'Kaput?'

'Entirely. We've no spares yet. They were sending them direct from the Leningrad factory.' Baugersky had kept himself to himself, but now it was the turn of his electrical department. 'We've got only one choice,' he added softly. 'To return to base for rewiring or to flog on south and live under impossible conditions.'

'Have you reported to the Old Man?'

'Thought I'd see you first. You understand the troops.'

Alexei smiled wryly. 'This will have the opposite effect on Lessner. You know his obstinacy. How can he explain away this latest sabotage? It would finish him.'

'And our friend, Grenz — he was sent here to cure this nonsense.' Georgiy slipped from the bunk. 'What are we going to do, Alexei?' he whispered. 'This is the worst yet. They're trying to force the ship home. We're on the edge of ... of...' He shook his head and made for the door. 'We're in for big trouble, Alexei. And we're just sitting on our arses. It's time Lessner woke up.'

Grenz, Baugersky and Slepak had confronted the captain in his cabin. Slepak was beginning to understand Lessner.

'How d'you know, Baugersky, that it was deliberate? Whatever caused the dead-short is now only a mess of molten metal. Could have been an accident — the dockyard, perhaps? The commissar agrees with me, don't you, Karl?' And so the interview had ended.

Lessner proceeded south, as soon as *Uranus* had fuelled. He reported the failure of the air-conditioning to C-in-C, Black

Sea, requesting that new armatures be despatched to Bissau. He asked Grenz to carry out an investigation but, in spite of Slepak's urging, decided not to speak again to the ship's company. 'Hard luck,' he had said. 'If everyone has to suffer in the heat of Guinea, the messdecks will be the worst off: they can work it out on the bastard who did it.' In the privacy of his cabin, he cursed: 'The shorting was deliberate. Drink, Number One? What's yours, Baugersky?'

'You're sure you won't address the ship's company again, sir?'

'No, First Lieutenant. I will not. They know exactly where they stand. This'll blow over, once they realize I and my officers mean business. Commander Grenz's investigation may give us something which we can pin on the ringleaders. We've only suspicions to go on — I reckon Leading Seaman Fomin is behind it all. I've been watching him — and so have you, haven't you, Commissar?'

Uranus slipped and set course for Cape Verde. Slepak realized that he was now entirely on his own. Several difficult choices lay before him, and he needed time to think things out. To clear his mind, he spent that afternoon walking round the upper deck, while *Uranus* dipped into the long Atlantic swell.

He tried to talk with the hands working on deck, but even the buffer was uncommunicative. He moved aft to the starboard quarter, which was in the shade. It was pleasant watching the flying-fish from here: the wash foamed in the blue sea; the last of the gulls wheeled silently across the stern; the blood-red ensign flapped above him.

Several hands were emerging up from the tiller flat behind him. He wandered for'd, not wishing to give the impression that he was loafing. He would find the buffer again: together they could draw up the work-routine for the next two days, while *Uranus* ploughed towards the Mauritanian coast.

COLLATOR'S NOTE 1

It is interesting to note Slepak's reference to his stumbling upon the hands gathered in the after-tiller flat on that Monday, 5 December. In his account of those vital days, he is strangely unaware of the significance of this first, clandestine meeting. If he had investigated further, he might have discovered the true state of things.

During my research, I traced and talked to one of those who was present in the tiller flat. The following is an extract from the tape which the witness kindly recorded for me:

'The news of the damage to the armatures came as a shock to us on the messdecks. To this day, I'm still not absolutely sure that one of us had done it — certainly no one owned up to it. All we knew was that we had gone too far. The hothead who'd done it had put us in the shit, sir. All we wanted was to get back home, get a decent ship, serve under a proper captain. We'd had our fill of Grenz, too. He had poisoned the lads. No one trusted nobody, see? So when the news of the burnt-out armatures hit us, we was buggered.' [The tape is distorted, but then the man continues]:

'It was Fomin, the leading hand, who suggested the meeting. He was always a crafty one, needling us, particularly the young 'uns, ever since them days in Kaliningrad. But he didn't want to be the leader, he said. Better to have a PO. So, after Korolev had refused (the chief MEA was in the engine room and we had to be quick about things, collecting together people off-watch), we asked Chief REA Litke if he'd take charge — he was a single man, sir, so to speak. Bitter, he was: wife had left him. We were always a bit afraid of him — underneath, he was chokka with the whole system. Anyway, he agreed and we held the meeting in the tiller flat as the ship steamed south off Mauritania. We was just coming up to the

Cape Verdes and it was hot as hell in the flat. Never forget it — for the first time, we realized the terrible hole we'd got ourselves into.'

Collator: 'Explain exactly what you mean.'

'Up to now, sir, the unrest had been the only way we could make them realize we were serious. But after Funchal, the troublemakers knew they couldn't draw back. They couldn't climb out of this one, if they was caught — and they knew Grenz well enough, with his bloody little Richter informing him all the time. The ringleaders knew they were bound to be dealt with eventually — shot or Siberia. So Fomin and the others, most of the young ones with no real responsibilities back home — they and the disillusioned men with nothing to look forward to in the Soviet Union — talked for the first time of their idea to take over the ship. It was the first time, sir ... just an idea, see?

'Fate ordained that Slepak should be a few minutes too late, or should be too gullible, when he noticed that mixed gathering emerging from the tiller flat. It is easy for us to criticize now: we must imagine the context of the days in which he was living — the tension, the uncertainty and loneliness, the terrible load he was bearing.'

— Derek Warne

CHAPTER EIGHTEEN

The first ten days in Bissau were the worst, while the crew acclimatized themselves to the humidity. The captain was rarely seen, spending most of his time either ashore with Grenz, or locked in his cabin composing ditties for his singsongs. Grenz was seldom available, having involved himself with the affairs of the locals by inveigling himself into the political morass that was now this African Republic. Slepak, to his relief, was left to run the ship.

Over a fortnight had already slipped by since *Uranus* had anchored in the darkness on the night of 13 December. On the next morning she had moved carefully up into the estuary, where she had lain at anchor in the muddy waters ever since. The boat routines had settled down, but the crews were beginning to feel the strain, even though the ship was working 'harbour routine' in three watches.

Prickly heat was the common lot of both officers and men, but until the spares for the air-conditioning fans came out, there was little that the doctor could do about his patients' condition, except to order a higher fruit-and-vegetable content in the diet, and more physical exercise.

The captain had granted daily leave from 1600 until 2200, when the last boat left shore. The ship's company's behaviour ashore had been good; duty 'one-in-three' gave them time to see something of the area, though they were ordered by the local authorities to remain within the town's boundaries — as much for their own safety as for any political reason. On the surface, things seemed serene in the ship after the Funchal incident, but Slepak felt the tension as intensely as ever: things were simmering between decks as dangerously as they ever had.

It was already 30 December and he had boobed. The coxswain, Korolev, had approached him on 22 December to ask if he, the first lieutenant, intended to lay on anything special for the traditional midday dinner on New Year's Day. The day was almost upon them, but Slepak had forgotten it in the flurry of his preoccupations. So Korolev, the cook and he had drawn up a special menu to vary the monotony of the diet which they had been enduring for so long. The coxswain and the storeman had gone ashore that day, 30 December, to organize the supplies which were to be collected from the jetty on New Year's Eve. The local robbers had suggested sucking pigs and the cook said he could cope. For booze, the captain had surprisingly agreed to a half-bottle of the local gut-rot for each man.

Slepak was leaning over the port wing of the veranda deck where he had gone to catch the breeze that had risen with the dusk. He watched the liberty-men mustering on the welldeck. There was a full turn-out tonight, fallen-in in two ranks while Perstev, the officer-of-the-day, inspected them. Alexei had signed several 'exchange-duty' chits during the day: several of the older hands had told him that they wanted to buy last-minute gifts to send home. Many among them had hoped to be with their families this year for New Year's Day. They were overdue for long leave, after over two years in *Uranus*.

'Permission to go ashore, sir?'

He turned and smiled at young Roman Surov, the sensitive and malleable fourth hand. His mother had come from Kazakhstan. He was a loner in the wardroom, partly because of Perstev's overbearing personality. Slepak liked Surov's conscientiousness and his friendliness. 'Carry on, Surov. Have a good run.'

'Thanks, sir. Can't persuade you to come too, can I?'

Alexei shook his head. 'Too much to do. I want to catch up on my mail.'

'Okay, sir. Goodnight.'

Slepak remained for the sunset and the short twilight. He enjoyed watching the first shore lights twinkling from the beach.

Then he remembered the ghastly evening before him: Lessner had laid on one of his sing-songs, but, mercifully, Grenz was still ashore. Alexei went below and washed for dinner. As the officers dragged themselves to the captain's cabin after the meal, he told Klavitter to inform Lessner that he could not attend. 'Present my apologies, Pilot. I've got too much work on, with the quarterly returns.'

To hell with the returns: a wave of tranquillity swept over him as he settled at his desk in the privacy of his cabin. He picked up his pen:

Uranus,
c/o Fleet Mail Office,
Sevastopol.
2110/30 December.

My beloved Katenka,

The mail leaves tomorrow, so you won't get this until after New Year's Day. But I can't let a mail slip past without writing a short note wishing you a Happy New Year; and to tell you what you know already: I love you, Katenka, with my whole being. I want to share my life with you, build a home, give you children. You know all this, I know, but sitting here in my stuffy cabin (the sweat from my forearms is sticking to the paper, it is so humid) I can see through my scuttle the yellow lights of Bissau twinkling along the shoreline. It is so sticky that it is difficult to resist sleeping on the upper-deck: a choice of two evils, but the mosquitoes — bigger even than those on the banks of the Pirita — are the largest and hungriest I have ever encountered.

I have borrowed a tape-recorder from the electrical lieutenant and beside me the music from Tchaikovsky's Pathétique *is gently playing, flooding my mind with memories of the happiest days of my life... Remember Kadriorg: the hot sand; our tent beneath the pines? (We have to censor the troops' mail, but officers are allowed to deal with their own; but the mail is again checked at a central office, I believe; there is so much I want to say to you.)*

Listen, Katenka — I'm going to marry you — as soon as I'm appointed to my 'long' course at Leningrad, so start looking for a flat — on the outskirts, but not too far from the Communications School, if you can find something. Two rooms will be more than enough for us, won't it? We'll see about the future later.

I can't tell you much about the ship and our movements. We're sweltering in Bissau. We don't know how long we'll be here — our stay depends on the political situation. (We can hear gunfire sometimes, during the daytime. The countryside is out of bounds to us, but we are allowed ashore in the town, so long as we stay within limits.)

There is a lot I'd like to tell you about Uranus. *(The sadness of this music is accentuating the loneliness, my Katenka.) It's hardly possible to be further away, is it? You, in the cold of a Russian winter; me, in this sweltering humidity. I am very much alone here. I can't say much more except that I am carrying an* enormous *load. I have the doctor, a delightful man; and Baugersky, the electrical officer whom I've already mentioned, as friends — but as for the rest! Too much now depends on me, on my judgement. One error on my part ... but I can't say more, except that I'll be glad when this is all over, one way or the other. Then I'll want to sleep for a week, away from it all — if you'll let me.*

Writing to you in these letters helps to banish the loneliness I feel. Your letters give me the strength I need. Keep writing.

Give my love to your parents and tell them I think of them constantly — and the future.

There's so much I want to talk to you about, fundamental things that we were beginning to discover together — particularly the mysteries posed that night by the Virgin of Kazan — remember? Through these matters of the spirit, my Katenka, we can stay close together, whatever the geographical distance that lies between us.

Goodnight, beloved.

Your Alyosha

As Alexei pounded the envelope with his censor's stamp, he heard the motorboat bumping alongside. The libertymen were in a rowdy mood tonight. He hoped Perstev would deal with them tactfully, even if there *were* a few drunks. A poke in an officer's eye at the moment was all that was needed to provoke the calamity that, in his mind, could occur at any moment.

He might have known it: New Year's Eve, fouled up before the day had even got underway. At breakfast, Perstev reported with evident satisfaction that he had run in three drunks. Their ebullience had disturbed the captain last night and, 'Captain's compliments, and would the first lieutenant please see them and place them in the Captain's Report for this morning?'

At the defaulters' table, the captain had been at his most insensitive, impatiently waiting for the coxswain to finish reading out the charges.

'I'll see them all together.' Lessner nodded at the first lieutenant.

'RO Lavisa; MEM Rykov; Ordinary Seaman Istomin — one pace forward — off caps,' Korolev snapped. 'Did at 2225 on Friday, 30 December, return on board drunk, sir.'

The three youngsters, pale and bleary-eyed, swept off their caps and stood at attention, glaring defiantly at their commanding officer.

The farce continued, Perstev confirming that he had found the three libertymen incapable of carrying out their duty.

'Anything to add, First Lieutenant?'

'No, sir, except that they give no trouble on board.'

Slepak sensed the presence of Rykov's divisional officer behind him. Melvedev, impatient to be off down to his engine room, had nothing to add on behalf of his rating, an insignificant, shifty-eyed stoker who was rarely seen on the upper deck.

'Nothing to say?' Lessner snapped at the defaulters.

The men shook their heads in silence. The captain was in one of his dangerous moods, his cheeks flushed, a scowl knotting his forehead.

'I won't have discredit brought on my ship.'

'Seven days' pay; seven days' leave stopped. On caps,' the coxswain barked. 'Dis-miss.'

The three defaulters turned right clumsily and began to shuffle away.

'*Come back here!*' Lessner was working himself up. 'Fall them in again, Coxswain. I'll have no more of this slovenliness. Dismiss properly.'

'Aye, aye, sir,' Korolev acknowledged wearily. 'Fall in again, you lot.'

Slepak felt nauseated by the performance. Fortunately, the commissar was not present to complicate matters.

Half an hour later, the quartermaster brought him a written memo from the captain: 'Captain's compliments, sir.'

So, communication now was by the written word? Lessner must have locked himself in again with his bottle. Alexei opened the buff envelope: 'From Captain,' he read aloud. 'To First Lieutenant. All shore leave and duty trips are stopped forthwith.' Alexei's stomach heaved with apprehension. 'The ship's company must be taught a lesson. I am not to be disturbed except in emergency.'

'Will that be all, sir?'

'Yes, Quartermaster. Carry on.'

The seaman turned, hesitated, then drew the curtain carefully across Slepak's doorway. He had wanted to speak, but Slepak had decided firmly that he would not talk directly with any of the hands, except through the official channels. He called after the departing seaman: 'Ask the coxswain to come and see me, please, Quartermaster.'

'Not even for the provisions?' Korolev was standing in Slepak's cabin. 'They're being delivered to the jetty tonight at 1800. What about our New Year's dinner tomorrow, sir?'

'Sorry, 'Swain. I've seen the captain again. The answer's "no". He insists that the hands learn from this lesson.'

'He'll be learning one too, if he doesn't watch out,' Korolev blurted. 'Sorry, sir.'

Their eyes met, the oldest rating in the ship and his executive officer. Slepak wanted to tell him of the embarrassing scene when he had defied Lessner, bearding him again in his cabin to try and convince him of the rashness of his decision, of the possible consequences. 'No, 'Swain. We'll have to make the best of it. We'll open up the dried fruits.'

'Cookie's preparing the meal now, sir. May I arrange with the buffer for a few hands to help with the spuds?'

'Of course. Do what you like, Cox'n.' Slepak added wearily: 'Try and explain it to the troops. The drunks are to blame.'

'If you say so, sir.'

'Cox'n.'

'Sir?'

'How bad is it — on the messdecks?'

Korolev shook his head. 'They keep me out of it, sir. But I don't like it. It's like a time-bomb ticking away down there.'

'Who's at the back of it?'

'Fomin, sir ... Salza ... and, well...'

'Go on.'

'Rather not say, sir. Can't be sure.'

Slepak hesitated, then smiled warmly. 'Okay, 'Swain. Do your best.'

'I will, sir.' The grizzled head shook ruefully. 'We'll have a bloody good nosh-up tomorrow, if I have to empty the pusser's store.'

The hands went about their work in sullen silence for the rest of the day. Their attitude was correct, but dumb insolence was difficult to combat. The dogwatches came and went, dusk settled and night closed in like a suffocating blanket. Grenz joined them for dinner, but even Perstev failed to respond to the commissar's forced conversation. The officers broke up in silence after the meal, each to his own cabin.

Slepak closed the door of his cabin behind him. He peered through the indigo hole that was his scuttle. He turned briskly, his decision made. He pulled the keyring from his pocket. As executive officer he was the only officer, besides the captain and the commissar, to have access to the confidential books locked in the safe which was welded to the bulkhead outside the wardroom.

Slepak walked quietly across the flat. He inserted the stainless steel key and turned the double locks. He searched through the mass of codes and ciphers and found the array of manuals. At the end, behind the Acts of War, was a slim volume in an unobtrusive brown cover. He glanced at the uninspiring publication: *Secret — For Officers' Use Only*. He slipped it into his reefer pocket, relocked the safe and stole back to his cabin. He slid the catch across his door. He settled in his chair, glanced again at the title and began reading.

He was still brooding over the contents when, shortly after one o'clock on New Year's Day, he heard a gentle scratching on his bulkhead. He stuffed the book beneath the mattress of his bunk. He tiptoed across the cabin, threw the catch and pulled open his door.

CHAPTER NINETEEN

It was already one-forty in the morning on New Year's Day, and so far, Doctor Nikolai Bogoraz had been unable to find sleep. He would resort to a pill: worry prevented him from sleeping, as much as the irritation of this prickly heat. He had shipped the torpedo-vent in his scuttle to scoop air into his cabin, but the effort was fruitless on this suffocating night. They were fools to have sabotaged the air-conditioning. He had tried to wheedle Fomin in secret, when the leading seaman had reported for treatment, but Fomin had immediately shied off. Fomin and Salza and...

Something was scraping against the ship's side, then suddenly there was a splash in the water. Feet were pattering on the deck above.

The doctor rolled from his bunk and slipped on his dressing gown. He slid through his open door and scrambled up the ladder. He moved silently through the screen door and approached the boat deck ladder — no sign of the quartermaster. He nipped up to the boat deck... Several shadowy forms were disappearing through the for'd screen, one of them undoubtedly Salza and the other, a tall, lean man — was that Leading RO Reek? Then he noticed lengths of cordage and flakes of white paint strewn on the deck. He glanced at the rail. He hurried silently down the ladders to the wardroom flat. He scratched on the bulkhead of number one's cabin.

In the semi-darkness he felt his heart racing. He was a medical man, not the stuff of which heroes are made. He was becoming a pawn in events which could lead only to tragedy.

Then he heard Slepak scuffling in his cabin. The door opened and he stepped inside, number one locking the door behind him.

'What's up, Kolya?'

Alexei was shoving the chair towards him. It was not surprising that they had selected Slepak to sort out this mess: there were cynical lines about his mouth, but he was a likeable chap, the main reason why the troops had so far remained relatively passive.

'They've ditched Klavitter's bike.'

'Say that again.'

'They've thrown the navigator's motorbike over the side.'

'How long ago?'

'Couple of minutes. I saw Salza and Reek clearing off. I couldn't prove it.'

The furrows deepened between Slepak's eyebrows. 'I was wondering what today would bring,' he murmured. 'It's got off to a good start.' He smiled ruefully and offered a cigarette. 'What else have you got for me, Kolya?'

'I'm in an impossible position,' Bogoraz said. 'The troops are my patients as much as you are. I respect their confidences, but often they are confiding in me so that I can leak information to the wardroom or, preferably, to you.'

'I understand, but I could do with a bit of help myself.' Slepak was facing him squarely, but those blue eyes were worried. 'What are Fomin and co. up to, Kolya? I can't let things slide any further.'

'That's why I'm here. The captain's totally ineffective and they can't stand Grenz. You're the only one they have any time for.'

Slepak smiled bleakly and stretched himself out on the bunk. 'Then why don't they put through their grievances in a proper service manner?' he asked.

'The majority want to do just that,' Bogoraz went on. 'But after your predecessor and the cox'n had been snubbed at Kaliningrad, and because of Lessner's arrogance in dealing with the troops, it was considered pointless risking further damage to their careers. But even now, the moderate faction would prefer to bring up their grievances properly, if they weren't overawed by the troublemakers.'

'What are their real grievances?'

Bogoraz drew deeply on his cigarette and watched the smoke curling towards the scuttle. 'Their main grouse, and to my mind an entirely justifiable one, is that at least eleven of the hands are overdue for long leave. Nobel, Nakhimov and Keyserling haven't been home for over two years. They'll be due to leave the service before they take their leave.'

'The buffer's in the same boat, but he doesn't make trouble.'

'He's a PO, Alexei — and "your" man. But there's a senior rating behind all this. He's being drawn more and more into it.'

'Litke — my Chief REA?' Alexei was missing nothing.

'Yeah, I reckon that Fomin has intentionally passed the buck to Mikhail Litke, now that they've overreached themselves. Fomin is a crafty devil — a ruthless schemer, manipulating the youngsters; they're putty in his hands. They look up to him as a seaman — and to Salza. They're afraid of them both. The Funchal sabotage has forced Fomin into a position from which he can't retract.'

'What are their other moans?' Slepak demanded.

'The usual: conditions on the messdecks; food; rotten mail service; being treated like infants for shore-leave — and the Old Man's sing-songs. It's the injustice which gets them down… Why *should* the officers keep the messdecks awake half the night? If the position was reversed…?' The doctor laughed bitterly. 'It's hardly edifying to be kept awake by bawdy songs half the night, several times a month, by officers whom you are supposed to respect. It's the injustices, the petty, arbitrary decisions, the restrictions — the whole damned unfairness.'

'Like the motorbike?'

'Between you and I, that's poetic justice. Klavitter's a bastard.'

'It doesn't help anyone.'

'Perhaps it's their final effort at convincing Lessner and the commissar that their easiest way out is to get the ship home — and, tacitly, to pardon the troublemakers,' the doctor said.

'They certainly chose the right night — when Grenz has stayed ashore with the political bosses. He's a mysterious sod.'

Bogoraz dropped his voice: 'I told you, didn't I, (and I'm not telling you who informed me of this) that Steward Richter bought a stereo from one of the hands in Klavitter's landing party at Izmir. Richter either gave it or sold it at a profit to Grenz — for services rendered, I'm assured.'

'Grenz is gay?'

'It's common knowledge on the messdeck. They know they're safe with Grenz.'

'Gentle blackmail — they'd finish his career?'

'They're trying to barter immunity from reprisals against Grenz's probity — a difficult operation for Litke, Fomin and co., under the circumstances. I've come to you for the last time, Number One, because I *know* that an explosive situation exists. The troops know that Lessner's useless, particularly during the forenoons. Raw, bloody mutiny can break out this morning, tomorrow, if YOU don't act fast.'

Alexei turned on his elbows to face him. 'Me?' he asked. 'What can I do?'

'You know bloody well, Alyosha. *You've* got to talk to the troops.'

Slepak dragged a small, brown book from beneath the mattress. 'Seen this?' He held up the confidential volume: *Mutiny: Action to be Taken by Officers.* He was unsmiling as he slipped from his bunk and threw back the door catch. 'I'll see the officers first thing after breakfast. Then I'll clear lower deck. Get some sleep, Kolya.'

Doctor Bogoraz crossed the flat and slipped silently through the door of his own cabin. He felt better, having shared his fears with Slepak. But tomorrow — today — would be decisive.

CHAPTER TWENTY

The difficulty would be Richter: how was he, Slepak, to rid himself of this unsavoury shadow while he addressed the officers? He would not yet issue the pistols.

At ten minutes past three on that Sunday morning of 1 January, Alexei Slepak wrote the memo to Grenz, informing him of the action he proposed to take. The first lieutenant was forced to move swiftly, because the captain declined to take any action, and because the commissar was not available. Slepak would dispatch Richter ashore in the morning boat to deliver the message by hand.

He fell into his bunk and slept until the steward shook him at seven.

At breakfast, the first lieutenant told Klavitter to assemble all the officers in the wardroom at 0845. Slepak personally asked the chief to be present and Melvedev had agreed without demur. Richter cleared the table, then went ashore in the motorboat to deliver the sealed envelope to Grenz.

Alexei Slepak brushed his hair and straightened the tunic collar of his number one suit. The face staring at him from the mirror above his washbasin was drawn and pale from lack of sleep. There were half-moon shadows beneath his bleary eyes. He knew that today, New Year's Day, would be decisive.

So much depended on the resolution of his wardroom brother officers, and particularly on the loyalty and attitude of Klavitter and Melvedev, the chief. The doctor and the electrical officer were stalwarts — but the chief? Disinterested, provided his engines ran smoothly. Klavitter? An enemy who would turn on his first lieutenant should things go wrong. Alexei Slepak braced his shoulders, grabbed his cap and strode across to the wardroom. He glanced at his watch: 0845 precisely. He shoved open the door.

He kept them standing. Klavitter had reluctantly risen to his feet; Maxim Melvedev, exceptionally in his number one suit, moved to Slepak's side; the doctor and Baugersky edged imperceptibly towards their first lieutenant. Perstev stood woodenly next to Klavitter; young Surov seemed bemused by the proceedings, his eyes darting from one officer to another.

'I've decided to speak to the ship's company,' Alexei said without preamble. 'The captain has declined to do so and has told me to get on with running the ship. The commissar is ashore. I'm clearing lower deck this forenoon, before any other incident overtakes us.' He glanced round at his silent audience, each apparently bewildered by the rapid surge of events. Klavitter was looking bored, contempt twisting his lips.

'I have told the coxswain to fall in the troops athwartships, in two ranks for'd of me and facing aft. I want you to form up behind me, for'd of me and facing aft. Allow me to do the talking, whatever happens. I'm not asking for advice, only your loyal support. I am deliberately not issuing pistols to you, but it may come even to that, later. If it does, each officer is responsible for his own weapon, which is to be used only in self-defence.' He saw the shock sweeping over Perstev and Surov's faces, as the gravity of the situation was forced upon them.

'Remember,' Slepak concluded, 'there are no bad troops — only bad officers. We're as much to blame as they are. I'm trying to halt the inevitable slide into disaster for us all. I need your support solidly behind me. That's all, gentlemen. I'll be clearing lower deck in five minutes' time.' He turned and left the wardroom for his cabin, where he sent for Korolev. 'Clear lower deck, Coxswain. Fall in the hands athwartships in two ranks and facing aft. I shall be addressing the ship's company.'

'Aye, aye, sir.' The coxswain smiled grimly and turned briskly on his heel. '*Aye, aye, sir*. Right away.'

Slepak watched him snatch the bosun's call from his pocket to make the pipe himself. He heard the call echoing along the upper deck, and shortly afterwards the patter of feet upon the steel overhead. He hoped the captain would be either asleep or too drunk to watch the proceedings on the welldeck. He put on his cap, brushed his suit and slowly climbed the ladder leading to the upper deck.

The officers were waiting for him by the passage door. He nodded to them, then walked for'd to the screen door where he waited, his officers in silence behind him. Through the half-clipped door he could hear the chiefs checking up on their divisions. He heard the coxswain's footsteps and then the sunlight was blinding them as Korolev swung open the door.

'Ship's company fallen in on the welldeck, sir.' He saluted and Slepak stepped out onto the blistering plates of the welldeck.

The two ranks were facing him, fallen in as he had ordered, the three chiefs and the petty officers a couple of paces in front.

'Ship's company ... *sshun*! ' the coxswain barked.

The hands sprung to attention. Slepak paused and caught sight of Fomin, Reek and Salza in the centre of the rear rank. He strode forwards briskly, turning at the last moment to the port side. He passed round the end of the ranks and halted, for'd of them and opposite the centre of the rear rank. He waited, the hands with their backs to him, for the officers to assemble behind him. Then he shouted the order himself.

'*Uranus* ship's company ... *a-bout turn*!'

Slepak saw the hesitant tremor in the ranks, heard the clatter of boots upon the deck — and then the forty-seven men were facing him.

Fomin, Salza and Reek were facing him, at less than two metres. They stood at attention, eyes directly before them, avoiding his scowl. Outmanoeuvred, they could not now surreptitiously cause trouble unobserved.

'Stand at ease, Coxswain.'

Slepak had not prepared his speech: for so many weeks he had brooded on the problem. He talked quietly with them, keeping down the temperature: there had been a mistake on all sides and he and his officers regretted them, as much as the lower deck did. Nothing could be gained by continuing this intensive war; nothing but terrible trouble could come to them all. They all knew the punishment for sedition, unrest and — he used the word precisely and without dramatics — mutiny. Things *could* be put right and he would himself see the commissar about past incidents. And for a long moment, he stared at the three ringleaders so close to him.

He promised to represent again their grievance regarding leave. The captain was sympathetic, but was up against the red-tape which they all realized snarled up the drafting offices.

Slepak deliberately fixed each junior rating with his eye. The men in the rear rank seemed restless, their eyes wandering to the three central figures now in the front rank.

Fomin turned his head once, trying to catch Litke's eye. But the chief REA remained frozen where he stood, unbalanced by the shift of events. There was silence on the welldeck; all were acutely conscious of their absent captain who must be watching through his cabin port.

Only a few faces reflected the hatred which had been seething for so long. Slepak no longer felt the uncertainty with which he had begun his address. They were listening to him, and Fomin and co. still had made no move. Slepak ended by emphasizing the loyalty which every man on board owed to the Service.

'We are all responsible to someone in authority directly above us,' he concluded. 'We all have to accept orders; even the commander-in-chief of the Soviet Navy has to carry out the directives of the central committee. The navy's a "big firm" to take on; it has a long arm, and you can never win.' He glanced directly at chief REA Litke, who was staring directly at Slepak. 'The object of my talking to you is quite simple: to prevent some of you from continuing down the treacherous route you have chosen. I don't want to hammer the point, but when it comes to fundamentals (perhaps the older hands will remember what happened to *Storozhevoy*), discipline has to be upheld. In the USSR, the Articles of War are not a feeble threat tucked away in a cupboard; the punishments, unlike the punishments in some of the world's navies, are precisely defined. Drunkenness receives "scale" and stoppage of leave; desertion or being absent-without-leave earns cells or imprisonment; and mutiny, the death penalty.'

Slepak heard a gull mewing and the wail of an ambulance siren drifting from ashore. No one stirred in the ranks before him; not a murmur, nothing but total silence.

'We all live by this code. Without total obedience, our navy could never have reached the position it has. We're the most powerful, most efficient navy in the world, bar the Americans; I and most of you standing before me intend that it should stay that way.' He nodded at Klavitter and snapped, 'Carry on the officers.'

He returned their salute. He met Fomin's stare and glanced at the enigmatic Litke in the rear.

'I wish you all a happy New Year's Day,' Slepak concluded, the twitch of a smile softening the lines on his face. 'Dismiss the ship's company, Coxswain.'

While he walked briskly towards the screen door, he heard them falling out. Their silence was worse than the outburst which he had expected.

CHAPTER TWENTY-ONE

The buffer appeared relieved when Slepak told him to work the hands lightly for the rest of the forenoon. Cleaning ship, squaring-off the upper deck and preparing the messes for the evening dinner would keep their minds off the traumatic start to the day.

The captain had ordered the motorboat for ten o'clock, when he went ashore to join Grenz: both had been invited to lunch with the Bissau hierarchy. Lessner had not referred to Slepak's talk, nor to the coming festivities of the evening. Grim-faced, he had stalked off the gangway, to the waiting motorboat manned by the port watch crew, the cox'n being Salza.

At 'stand-easy', Alexei took his coffee in the wardroom. The conversation was stilted, and Klavitter provided a jarring note. The doctor and Baugersky had approached Slepak inconspicuously to tell him that the talk had been exactly what was required. The chief had stood on the side-lines, a sarcastic smile on his face.

'Pity you had to put the blame on the officers,' Klavitter blurted. 'With respect, Number One, I thought you went too far. You didn't have to crawl to 'em.'

Perstev rose from the settee to stand by Klavitter. His jaw was set, a veritable Captain Bligh.

'Have you finished, Pilot?' Slepak snapped, banging his cup on the table.

'No, Number One. I resent your assumption of command. I'm responsible to my captain and, thank God…'

'Yes, Klavitter?'

The navigator was glaring round the wardroom, seeking support. 'I think you've gone too far. You're as bad as the troops — disloyal. I prefer Grenz's methods to yours.'

'Shut up, Klavitter.' Baugersky seized the navigator's elbow. 'You're an arrogant snob and the cause of most of our troubles. Your great-grandfather may have been a Latvian shipbuilder, but that doesn't give you the licence you assume. I'm sick of your disloyalty to number one.'

'That goes for me, too,' the doc added quietly. 'But let's stop this bickering.' He jerked his head towards the pantry-hatch. 'Number One did bloody well.'

'We ought to stick by the first lieutenant,' the nervous voice of Surov cut in. 'I know I'm the new sprog here, but I think the troops are on the edge of ... of...'

'Go on, say it,' Perstev sneered. 'You don't dare? You'd be the first to be on their side. You're always sucking up to the senior ratings. The pilot's right; you've got to be tough with 'em.'

'I'll be seeing Grenz when he comes back on board,' Klavitter said blandly, lighting up another cigarette. 'With your permission, *of course*?' He glared insolently at his first lieutenant.

Slepak felt the anger mounting inside him. He should order Klavitter to his cabin until Lessner returned... Then he heard the pipe. 'Out pipes — carry on with your work.' There was a knock on the door; Chief REA Litke's pale face was peering through the curtain.

'First Lieutenant, sir?'

'Come in, Chief.'

'Secret and immediate, sir.'

Slepak moved aside from Klavitter and took the proffered signal file. 'From C-in-C, Black Sea, to *Uranus* Repeated *Zemlya*,' he said. 'Immediate: on completion of fuelling, you are

to proceed a.m. 2 January at cruising speed to position 235° —
Boa Vista, Cape Verde Islands — 250 miles, to arrive 1100
(ZT) 5 January. NATO exercises confirmed to be moving into
South Atlantic. Shadow and report. AGT *Zemlya* will
rendezvous with you a.m. 6 January. Acknowledge.' Slepak
handed back the board. 'Thank you, Chief. Well, that settles a
lot of our problems.' He addressed Surov. 'Take a copy of this
signal ashore and show it to the captain.' He turned to Litke.
'Hoist the General Recall, please. You're the OOD, Pilot? Send
in the motorboat right away with the fourth hand. Tell the
coxswain to wait — Salza, isn't he?'

'Yes,' Klavitter growled. 'You'll excuse me? Duty calls.' The
chief and Baugersky remained with the first lieutenant in the
wardroom. There was much to arrange if the ship was to be
ready by 1100 tomorrow — and 1 January was not the easiest
of days on which to lay on demands with shore-side.

Alexei snatched a moment at the end of the forenoon in which
to write to Katya:

*A last-minute scrawl, to tell you we are on our way again. I'm getting off
a mail this afternoon, so hope this reaches you soon. Still haven't had a
letter from you. I worry about you when I don't hear. I can't help fearing
the worst. Write, my Katenka, write quickly. I miss you and I long to
have you to myself again, once we get out of this mess. I think I may have
got on top of things. I certainly pray to your unknown God that I have:
the alternative is too terrifying to contemplate. I miss you. I love you. I
want you. Alexei.*

And as he imprinted the censor's stamp upon the envelope,
the coxswain rapped on the door-lintel. 'See you a moment, sir,
please?'

'Come in, 'Swain. Land the postman in the last boat, please. Warn the troops about the mail — and shove this in the bag, will you? What can I do for you?'

'May I have a few hands to help Cookie this afternoon, sir? He'll be needing a hand with the spuds and the dried stores, now that we've got to use our own provisions...' Korolev smiled for the first time that Slepak could remember.

'Course, 'Swain. See the buffer.'

'There's something else.' He produced a coloured drawing from his pocket. 'This went up on the officers' noticeboard, after you spoke to the hands. But before I had time to deal with it, I found it on my office desk. Sorry about it, sir. Most of us agreed with you. What you said was right, sir.'

'Thanks.' Slepak stretched out his hand for a further cartoon by the messdeck artist. The same acid, crude wit: a sow, a *Uranus* cap-ribbon about her snout, was suckling a solitary piglet from her gross teat. There were two stripes on each of the piglet's forelegs and along its back was stencilled: *Jimmy-the-One*. The caption read: *Sucking up gets you nowhere.*

'Clever — but not funny.' Slepak handed back the cartoon. 'I'm sorry too, 'Swain. I hoped they had accepted what I said.'

'Some hothead, sir. It was taken down after stand-easy.'

'Forget about it. Let's hope tonight's jollity will cure the sickness.'

'Wish I was as hopeful as you, sir. There's a nasty feeling on the messdecks.'

The humidity was worst during the afternoons. Most of the officers and men had their heads down, but Klavitter had gone up to the bridge to prepare tomorrow's passage. Slepak decided to show an interest in the preparations for the dinner — and at the same time he wanted to meet the Old Man at the gangway, if he came off unobtrusively. The flags for the General Recall hung limply from the spur crosstrees; Perstev and the quartermaster were sheltering in the shade of the small awning which had been rigged on the veranda deck. Slepak would start his rounds in the galley and try to cheer up the cook and his merry men. He glanced at his watch: 1520 — all good men should have their heads down.

He strolled down to the main deck, intending merely to show an interest. He stood silently by the doorway of the torrid galley. Cast iron saucepans strewed the ranges. The white-capped cookie moved neatly about his galley, captain of his own ship, a couple of seamen and stewards chiakking him as he pottered.

At the after end, out of sight of the casual passer-by, a group of men was crouched around a stack of potatoes. Slepak was about to enter when he became aware of the composition of the volunteers: Fomin was there, with Reek and Salza. Wasn't he duty boat's coxswain? But the motorboat had just been sent in to collect the captain. Salza must have persuaded Leading Seaman Voikov, the starboard watch coxswain, to substitute for him. *Curious that Salza should prefer to peel spuds*, thought Slepak. There were several others, about a dozen in all, and, in their centre, bent low over the mounting heap, was the tall, gaunt figure of the chief REA. What the hell was Litke doing there? Or was he showing the hands his usual flair for leadership? Slepak stepped backwards and returned to his cabin.

He locked his door and lay motionless on his bunk, staring up at the mottled patchwork of light criss-crossing the deckhead.

COLLATOR'S NOTE 2

Slepak's awareness of the significance of the curious composition of volunteers in the galley is substantiated by the same man who told me of the original tiller-flat meeting. The witness was himself in the galley, helping the cook with the soup and the sauces. He, too, was surprised by the constitution of the spud-peeling volunteers. He could only guess their intentions, but he realized later that this must have been the vital meeting when the terrible decision was finally taken. My witness is certain that the ratings he has named were present, and subsequent events bear out his testimony. The following, he asserts, were in the 'volunteer' party: Chief REA Litke, in the centre of the group; Leading Seaman Fomin; Leading RO Reek; MEA Nobel; Leading RO Yanov; Leading MEM Nakhimov; Able Seaman Salza, Ordinary Seamen Zubov and Vize; Keyserling, Torah, Chalidze (the youngest man on board) and Arbatov; MEMs Rostropovich, Rykov, and the Estonian, Lange, the youngest in the engine room department.

It is therefore almost certain that Litke and his three henchmen, Fomin, Salza and Reek, took the irrevocable decision at this second meeting. The morning's signal had determined their immediate further action: they had to gain time in which to agree among themselves the tactical decisions in order to achieve their objectives; and they needed time to try and persuade more of their messmates to join them. From now on, they were committed; secrecy was paramount, loyalty to their cause, literally, a matter of life or death.

But it must have been Richter, the steward, who informed Litke that the first lieutenant had witnessed their clandestine meeting.

— Derek Warne

The end of that amazing New Year's Day would remain in their minds for as long as they lived. Alexei Slepak certainly would never forget it.

The captain's boat came off at 1705. In it was a jovial Lessner, complete with the ship's company booze ration; he had at the last moment relented. But no Commissar Grenz. Another boat had to be sent in for him; when he arrived on board, he was twenty minutes late for the wardroom dinner.

The atmosphere at the dinner table was electric, everyone — except for Klavitter and Perstev, who sat glaring at each other across the table — doing their utmost to return to normality. The wardroom cook had done his best: turtle soup; frozen cod, fried in bread crumbs; curried meatballs; stewed dried figs and apricots; black coffee. The fiery local plonk aided the meal, and even Grenz began to thaw. He had been secretive about his dealings with the locals. The vodka was being broached, the steward approaching the captain at the table, when the coxswain, a nervous smile creasing his weasel face, poked his head round the door. 'Captain, sir,' he asked, 'ship company's compliments, but would you and the officers have "sippers" with us? We'd like to wish you the "Top of the Season", if you understand what we mean, sir.' He smiled sheepishly.

Lessner rose from the table to shake the coxswain's hand. Then Korolev led the procession to the chiefs' mess, where began the ceremony of toasting the new year, one mess after the other. Where the vodka had originated, no one asked. Grenz was red with confusion and booze, bewildered utterly by the mercurial temperament of simple sailors. Even the older hands became maudlin; the youngsters, brashly familiar; and the remainder oblivious to everyone and everything. They needed to sing.

'Will you lead us up on the upper deck, sir?' Chief REA Litke asked his captain. 'It's cooler up there.'

Slepak was watching carefully. Lessner was a child in Litke's hands. The chief REA had not taken one drink, but was smiling sardonically to himself. The cox'n sent for the emergency lights; the buffer set off towards the for'd screen door and then began the amazing spectacle.

The coxswain led the procession around the upper deck.

Harmonizing their favourite folk songs in their splendid Russian voices, the fifty-six officers and men of AGI *Uranus* snaked around the upper deck, lanterns swinging rhythmically to the traditional tunes. The reflections from the lights danced on the black water; the harmony echoed into the night. Up to the fo'c'sle head, down the starboard side, back to the boat deck, aft to the monitoring offices, down to the poop-deck and back up the port side until they returned again to the welldeck.

Slepak felt, for the first time, a feeling of affection for the ship in which he and all of them served. Even Klavitter was taking part; young Surov was harmonizing with Litke, and the buffer was conducting his own bass group. The captain was grinning foolishly; Grenz was joining in, his eyes everywhere, missing nothing. They hoisted Lessner onto the crane pedestal.

'*All our officers!*' someone cried.

To Slepak's astonishment, Grenz, and then himself, Baugersky, the doc and the others were handed up to the crane platform. Alexei looked down at the sea of faces peering up at them, the troops cheering at the top of their voices. He found it difficult to believe this incredible transformation was taking place. The buffer was leading the chorus: '*For they are jolly good fellows.*' They roared it at full volume, the words echoing into the night. Fomin (Alexei thought it was he) proposed three cheers; the hurrahs over, the officers were helped down to the deck. The captain shook hands with the coxswain; Grenz with Litke; Klavitter with Fomin — and Slepak with the buffer and Korolev.

The coxswain piped 'lights out' and, still happily singing, the officers and men of *Uranus* turned in for the night.

Peace and quiet settled over the ship. She swung to her anchor, the gurgling of the current against her cable the only sound in the darkness of the heavy, oppressive night.

CHAPTER TWENTY-TWO

Reality returned all too soon during the morning of 2 January: heat, hangover and hard work reduced the *bonhomie* that had blossomed the night before. On weighing at 0730, *Uranus* picked up a foul anchor which took over half an hour to free from the bight of rusty wire. She went alongside the fuelling jetty, then slipped at 1100.

Alexei was on the bridge, having reported 'secured for sea.' It was good to feel the ship's own wind again. The jumble of broken down shacks and shore installations glided past as *Uranus* worked up to her cruising speed. The south bank of the Geba River was out of sight on the southern horizon, but it was over two hours before the ship cleared the swirling, muddy waters of the estuary. By dinner time, the first low-lying blur of the Bissagos Archipelago hove in sight on the port bow.

The hands needed a break, in Slepak's judgement, so he piped a 'make-and-mend'. No work for the afternoon: those who so wished could get their heads down, an exercise of which Grenz disapproved sarcastically to the captain, within Slepak's hearing. Alexei shrugged his shoulders impatiently and went below: it was no business of Grenz's how the first lieutenant worked the hands. He fell into a deep sleep, vital if he was to keep his morning watch efficiently and if he was to train the fourth hand properly.

He returned to the bridge at 1830 to enjoy the cool of the evening. The Bissagos Archipelago was already abaft their beam, and Klavitter had set a course of 267° for the rendezvous with *Zemlya*. At *Uranus*'s cruising speed of 13 knots, she would arrive on her billet at 0830 on the morning of

Thursday, 5 January, *Zemlya* being expected on the sixth. Surov, Klavitter's 'tanky' (he helped with the navigational chores) was replacing the books on the shelf above the chart table. When Slepak asked to see the chart, Surov enthusiastically demonstrated the planned passage.

Tuesday's dawn, 3 January, was muggy and overcast. Slepak handed over his watch to the forenoon officer of the watch, Perstev, who had recently earned his watchkeeping certificate. The first lieutenant left the bridge, Surov following him. A shave, wash and strong coffee were needed to restore morale. The troops, too, needed a spell of stability and a regular, uncomplicated routine. The communications department seemed happy, working efficiently at their routine monitoring and dealing with the uncomplicated traffic coming in over the ether. The deck hands were docile as they worked silently at their chores, overhauling the gear; Petty Officer Vritsky was glad of a few quiet days in which to bring the ship up to scratch again after her long spell in harbour.

'If you are on top of your work, Buffer, we'll stick to sea routine. Pipe "make-and-mend" at dinner.'

At noon, Slepak climbed to the bridge to await Grenz's reaction. In this trial of strength, Slepak had no intention of allowing the commissar to interfere with the first lieutenant's authority. 'Hands to dinner,' the pipe shrilled over the intercom. 'Hands to make-and-mend clothes.'

Grenz was in a huddle with Lessner in the port wing, when the call shrilled over the speaker. Slepak watched the stocky figure stiffen as the captain beckoned.

'First Lieutenant.'

'Sir?' Alexei saluted.

'You granted a make-and-mend yesterday.'

'Yes, sir.'

'Don't you think you're overdoing it? What about the rust on the gunwales which I pointed out to you? The ring of chipping hammers would do us all a power of good.'

'I've considered it, sir, but I'm on top of the work.'

'The commissar considers that you're being too lenient with the hands. He's my political adviser.'

Chief REA Litke had approached them silently with the midday batch of signals. He stood aside, waiting for the conversation to end.

Grenz cut in: 'Yes, Captain, I do insist. The first lieutenant's got to be tougher. If he'd been stricter, we should not have suffered the few troubles we've had. That's my frank opinion, Captain. I was sent to *Uranus* to bring her back to fleet standards. I have to make my report at the end of the month.'

Lessner's eyebrows rose. He stroked his unshaven chin, almost beseeching his first lieutenant to haul him out of the mess.

'I disagree entirely with your commissar, sir,' Slepak snapped, as Grenz hunched his shoulders. 'Unless you order me to cancel the pipe, sir, I shall continue with the make-and-mend.' Slepak watched the anger simmering in Grenz's black pupils beneath his half-closed lids.

'Cancel your make-and-mend, First Lieutenant,' the captain ordered quietly, so that Litke could not hear. 'The hands are to work this afternoon.'

'Chipping and scraping,' Grenz added, a half-smile twitching his thin lips.

Slepak saluted his captain, then turned on his heel. As he strode through the wheelhouse, he ordered, 'Make the following pipe: make-and-mend is cancelled. Hands will fall in at 1400 to work ship.'

He scuttled down the ladders to his cabin. He flung his cap onto his bunk; he peeled off his shirt and grabbed his towel to mop up the sweat running down his body.

The rattle of chipping hammers rang round the ship during that afternoon, Tuesday, 3 January. At 1530 the coxswain was summoned to the captain's cabin. Slepak was not invited, until the petty officers were also hauled up to the Old Man's cabin. Lessner asked them for their views, but, to a man, they returned only evasive and innocuous replies. As they departed, they studiously avoided Grenz, who was standing between the captain and the door.

'What do you make of that, Commissar?' Lessner asked, his face drained of colour. 'The cox'n has convinced me.'

'Issue pistols to the officers, Captain. As I told you, that's the only sort of persuasion they'll understand.'

Lessner turned to Slepak: 'Draw the pistols from the rack — one to each officer. I've got my own.'

Slepak hesitated. So it had come to this?

'Carry on, First Lieutenant.'

Slepak walked past Grenz. He left the cabin, leaving the door open behind him.

Tuesday night drifted into the morning of Wednesday, 4 January. When Slepak took over the morning watch from Perstev, Surov seemed to be more immersed than usual in the navigation. *Uranus* was well into the Atlantic and the fourth hand was keen for Alexei to show him how to lay off a rhumb-line course; he had even extracted the small-scale charts of the northern mid-Atlantic Ridge. So the watch passed, and Wednesday dawned.

The officers reluctantly carried their revolvers. In the fresh light of this new day, to Slepak's eyes the offensive weapons were an ostentatious provocation, strapped around the waists of the officers. Alexei and Surov had deliberately removed their belts during the watch and they chattered more than usual with the quartermasters, Salza and Zubov.

The heat was oppressive at midday, in spite of the ship's thirteen knots, and Slepak did not visit the bridge when dinner was again piped at noon. To avoid misunderstanding, the ship's company was reminded that it would be working ship again at 1400. And during that sweltering afternoon, the first lieutenant was seen about the upper deck, checking here, inspecting there, talking to the hands. He sensed the resentment which the pistol, dangling in its holster at his side, created wherever he went.

Slepak was thankful when eventually at 1630 the hands returned gear and finished off their work. He stayed away from the wardroom and took his supper as early as possible. Four o'clock the next morning, 5 January, would arrive all too soon and he craved sleep. This would be his last watch but one before *Uranus* arrived in position for her rendezvous with *Zemlya*, which was to take place during the following forenoon, Friday, 6 January.

He must remind Litke to be ready with the transmission of the position report: Admiralty did not like being kept waiting. Slepak unhitched his pistol belt, shoved the cumbrous paraphernalia into his wardrobe, slipped into pyjamas and crawled into his bunk.

COLLATOR'S NOTE 3

Those who live ashore cannot begin to imagine what a cataclysmic decision a man takes when he decides to mutiny. His decision is irrevocable. From thenceforward, it is a fight to the finish against the colossal apparatus of the State.

The mutineer is gambling with his life: he must *win. Perhaps it is this polarization of choice which causes the savagery for which mutinies are notorious?*

My same witness has described the atmosphere in the messdecks as 'horrible', 'terrifying' and 'a tension you could feel wherever you went.' The ringleaders had to be sure of their men: they could approach only those who might reasonably be expected to join them, and my witness, being a single man and a bit of a wanderer, described to me how he had agreed to throw in his lot with the troublemakers. He had asked for detailed plans as to the future, but Fomin, who was doing most of the clandestine campaigning, had replied that they, the 'executive committee' as they called themselves, would take all the 'comrades' into their confidence when the moment was right.

Needless to say, this sedition, with so much at stake, had a highly divisive effect on the messdecks. The committee had to take its final decision and then act swiftly, before rumour spread to the officers — or before they were betrayed by a possible informer from the lower deck.

That night, Wednesday, 4 January, after supper, the committee assembled for the last time in the tiller-flat, to take final decisions — or, as my witness put it, 'to give us our marching orders, simply and precisely.'

— Derek Warne

CHAPTER TWENTY-THREE

There was no moon on that early morning of Thursday, 5 January. Slepak felt only half-awake as he took over the watch from Perstev. He would let Surov take most of the weight for once — the responsibility would do him good.

The green glow from the binnacle highlighted the high-boned features of the quartermaster, that tough old loner, Able Seaman Salza. The Old Man had insisted on keeping the steering 'in hand' instead of using the automatic pilot, so that seamen could learn how to steer. 'They don't know the feel of a wheel these days.' There was sense in the captain's opinion. Then Slepak remembered his pistol. 'Surov,' he called from the port wing. 'Here, a moment.'

The tall silhouette of the fourth hand loomed up in the darkness.

'Nip down to my cabin,' Slepak murmured (the port lookout was wedged into the corner of the bridge screen). 'Bring up my pistol. I've left it in the bottom of my wardrobe. Bloody stupid of me.'

Surov seemed to hesitate; then he saluted and clattered down the ladder to the boat deck. He had said nothing, embarrassed perhaps by his superior officer's apparent irresponsibility.

Slepak took off his cap and let the breeze blow through his hair. That was better: he hated these tropics. Then the memories of a Leningrad winter came flooding back.

'Number One, sir,' Surov was whispering by his side, 'your gun's missing.'

At that moment (0414 by the bridge clock — a time that Slepak would never forget) Captain Felix Lessner arrived on the bridge — unusual for him at this hour.

'Where are we, Number One?' he hailed from the chart table at the after end of the bridge. 'We ought to be entering the northern end of the South Equatorial Current any time now.'

Slepak was reaching the binnacle and crossing to the chart table, when he heard behind him the siren lever jerking against the screen. Three blasts suddenly boomed above them in the night. He collided with the captain as they both rushed for the doorway. As he stepped outside into the darkness, he heard the *ting* of the telegraphs, as the engines were ordered full astern by the quartermaster.

Slepak was the first to stumble through the door. Surov loomed in front of him, a pistol gleaming in his fist.

'Sorry about this, Number One.'

Slepak's arms were suddenly pinioned behind him, as two shadowy figures pounced from behind the screen.

'Take him inside,' Surov commanded. 'Watch over him, Torah.'

Prodded in the back by Surov's gun, Slepak was forced back into the wheelhouse. Lessner had drawn his pistol. He was swivelling on his heel and aiming at the indistinct forms rushing towards him. 'So it's you, Fomin, you bastard!' There was the crack of a shot, an orange flash and someone fell screaming. The rattle of an automatic shattered the calm of the wheelhouse. The captain dropped, writhing, to the deck. Fomin, the barrel of his gun smoking, stood over him, the steel jabbing the nape of Lessner's neck.

At that instant, the ship's intercom system came to life. A bosun's call shrilled; Litke's voice was issuing through the speakers, Litke's cool, authoritative words addressing the ship's company, broadcasting presumably from the gangway position. As he spoke, the ship began shuddering as her engines gathered full stern power: 'D'ye hear there? *Stand-by to abandon ship... Stand-by to abandon ship*. All hands muster in the well-deck. *At the rush*!'

The hull was vibrating fiercely as the bewildered men off-watch stumbled sleepily for'd. Slepak watched through the bridge windows as the hands arrived on the well-deck, bemused, then scared as they faced the levelled barrels of automatics held by their determined messmates.

'Get fell in,' Litke snapped over the speakers. 'Do as you are ordered, and no one will get hurt. Try anything stupid and you'll be gunned down without mercy. You'll be interested to know that Grenz has just shot Istomin in the back.'

Lessner was moaning at Fomin's feet. A dark patch welled across the wheelhouse deck as the seconds ticked by. Salza had picked up the pistol which Fomin had kicked from the dying captain's hand. Lessner was staring at his first lieutenant. He was trying to speak, but the words were unintelligible as his blood began to drown him.

'Stop the engines,' Litke ordered over the intercom. He went on in his assured voice: 'Now that you're mustered, you are to march in single file, down the port passage and up to the boat deck. The second motor cutter has been lowered to the rail. Man the boat in silence, without fuss. We have you covered every inch of the way. *Now — move*!'

Fomin was dispatching Lessner by putting a bullet through the back of his skull. Slepak turned away as the shot echoed through the wheelhouse. 'The bugger's dead,' Fomin said. Salza had switched on the bridge intercom system and the report echoed on the welldeck. The ranks were already on the move, but they wavered momentarily from the shock of the killing. Then they started filtering swiftly through the screen door.

'Get on deck, Number One.' Surov's arm hung at his side, the gun idle in his hand. 'Torah's guarding you.'

Slepak watched the amazing sight from the port wing: first the port watch, then the starboard, meekly manning the boat waiting at the rails. The dark shapes of the armed men were tucked into every vantage point. The last man was finally squeezed into the motor cutter.

'I'm lowering you halfway,' the invisible Litke snapped again through the speakers. 'Wait there in silence while we fetch the officers.'

The falls squealed. The boat was lowered halfway to the water. Slepak could see the packed heads massed in the boat which was swinging to the slow roll of the ship.

'Fetch the officers!' Once again the incisive voice of Litke. Alexei heard behind him the thud of Lessner's head across the tracks of the wheelhouse door as Fomin and Salza dragged the body to the wings. 'Give us a hand, sir.' Fomin glanced up at Surov. 'He's bloody heavy.'

'Torah, you can help.' Surov spoke softly, then levelled his pistol at Slepak's chest.

'You bastard,' Slepak whispered. 'You disloyal bastard.' He heard the click as the safety catch was released. Even in this half-light, Surov's face looked scared and white. 'Keep silence, Number One,' he whispered, 'if you want to stay alive.'

In full view of the crammed lifeboat, Salza, Fomin and Torah toppled the corpse over the side. The body slithered down the ship's plating and bounced across the rail, then on the rubbing strake. The phosphorescence sparkled as the corpse splashed into the dark waters.

'That was your captain,' Litke broadcast.

No one moved in the waiting boat. Several embarrassed cheers rang from the darkest corners of the upper deck.

'Stand-by the officers. Slide down the lifelines,' Litke ordered. 'Go on, Perstev, what are you waiting for?'

Slepak instinctively began to move towards the ladder. Would they wait for him?

'Stop where you are, Slepak. You're not going.' Fomin, still fondling the automatic, was barring the way to the ladder.

Perstev was manning the boat, one leg over the rail. The doctor was leaning outboard and was clutching the lifelines held by Baugersky; Melvedev, the chief, had slid halfway down his rope, his lifejacket a vast balloon, as he disappeared into the outstretched arms. There remained only Klavitter, who was struggling in the grip of three men.

He broke free suddenly and grabbed the automatic which an unsuspecting sentry was holding. He spun round. The gun flashed, stuttered and men began to fall.

Slepak watched helplessly as someone, who was standing in the shadows behind Klavitter, wrenched the axe from its stowage by the fire main. It was Reek, stepping from the darkness, who swung the long-handled axe. Slepak heard Klavitter's scream and the crunch of the smashed skull as the navigator slumped lifeless to the deck.

There was another splash when they hurled the body into the water. The falls began to squeal again.

'Slip the boat!'

Then, as the familiar sound of the hull crashing into the water reached Slepak's ears, Litke was issuing his final orders: 'You're not far from the shipping lanes. You've got enough food and water for several days. As soon as we're clear of the area, we'll put out a Mayday for you. So long, comrades. Good luck — and long live freedom!'

There was a burst of cheering from the dark upper deck.

'Full ahead both engines,' Litke ordered.

Surov ran into the wheelhouse. The telegraph clanged. The ship trembled as she gathered way. The cries dimmed as the lifeboat became a blur, then disappeared swiftly into the night.

CHAPTER TWENTY-FOUR

Slepak watched the dawn lightening through the scuttle of what had been his cabin but was now his prison. Outside the door a sentry paced, so Slepak stretched himself out on his bunk to think. There was little else he could do.

He was still shocked by the rapidity of the appalling events: in minutes, his world had been toppled. Litke and his henchmen had organized the mutiny with incredible precision.

They had depended upon the docility of their messmates, but perhaps had been surprised by the resistance from the officers they had killed. Slepak still felt revolted by Fomin's butchery of Lessner; of Klavitter's brains splattered against the grille of the engine room fan intakes. Of Grenz he had heard nothing, except that they had locked him in the for'd cell. He had shot down the youngest member of the ship's company, the wretched Istomin; in the mutineers' present mood, the commissar stood little chance. Of those whom Klavitter had sprayed with the automatic, how many had been killed or maimed? In the general panic, the mutineers had condemned the doctor to the lifeboat: they must be regretting the decision. The POs were trained in first aid, but they were no more knowledgeable than Slepak.

He raised himself on his elbow to stare through the scuttle as he felt the ship heel from the turn she was making. His cabin was on the starboard side; he had not glimpsed the sun, so *Uranus* must be southward bound. What the hell was Litke up to? He may have taken over the ship, but what could be his intentions now? Steaming in circles halfway between Africa and South America would get him nowhere, and the fuel could not last forever.

The castaways would be all right, with reasonable luck. Though the boat was crammed to the gunwales, they had plenty of water and food, Litke said. They were on the edge of the shipping lanes, so should be sighted soon, even if *Zemlya* failed to find them when trying tomorrow to rendezvous with the missing *Uranus*.

Surov ... the naive, inexperienced Surov, whom Slepak had helped in the long morning watches. Alexei felt saddened by the fourth hand's disloyalty, but there must have been some terrible motive for him to defect, something of which Slepak knew nothing. Presumably Surov was navigating now. If Surov had not been on the bridge at the moment of mutiny, what chance would he, Slepak, have stood?

And what of his own future? Would they butcher him also? There was nothing that he could do, so he might as well wash and shave. When he could reason more clearly, he would try to fathom how the mutineers hoped they could get away with this piracy on the high seas. If the fate of *Storozhevoy*'s crew was anything to go by, the future for Litke's mutineers was not bright. But the Atlantic was not the Baltic.

Slepak would get as much sleep as he could. When he awoke, he would bring his diary up to date. He would wrap it, with a couple of pencils, inside a length of terylene sailcloth which he had in his drawer. While he was alive, no one would take that from him. He had promised it to Katenka; only she was to have it.

COLLATOR'S NOTE 4

The typewritten sheets terminate at this point, the remainder of the manuscript being in an erratic longhand.

From the evidence of my witness (now one of the mutineers), Litke, Fomin, Salza and Reek had been amazed by the comparative ease with which they had captured the ship. There was now disagreement as to what should be done with the two prisoners, Grenz and Slepak, but there was complete accord with their prime objective.

They would take the ship to the nearest point off South America, Ponta de Calcanhar, Brazil. At sixteen knots, Uranus would have plenty of fuel in hand. If Surov could find the group of islands, the Archipelago Fernando de Noronha, even he could not fail to make a landfall somewhere near Fortaleza, Natal or Recife — provided he missed the Rocas. The mutineers would scuttle the ship in deep water, just outside territorial waters.

The remaining motor cutter would land them on a deserted beach of their own choosing. They could sink the boat if necessary, then claim political asylum as shipwrecked mariners. Brazil was a good choice politically. In this huge and friendly country, they could all start new lives.

The mutineers steamed the ship on her south-south-westerly course, each revolution of the ship's propellers taking them nearer to safety. The vital requirement was to put as much distance as possible between Uranus's *rendezvous with* Zemlya, *due during the forenoon of Friday, 6 January.* Zemlya *would take time to raise the alarm, provided she did not pick up the castaways' boat. The Atlantic was a big ocean.*

To assure normality, Litke kept the routines going, transmitting at the ordered times, the majority of his ROs having joined the mutineers. On the second day, after pushing out an anonymous Mayday during the morning of the sixth, he personally pulled the transmitter fuses and threw them over the side.

Leading MEM Nakhimov ran the engine room. There were enough MEMs (Rostropovich, Rykov and the Estonian, Lange) to keep two watches. The diesels were giving no trouble; it was a matter of keeping things going for five days when they would make their landfall.

Their besetting fear was that Admiralty might immediately lay on a massive search, but in one respect they stood a good chance: as far as anyone knew, there were no long-range reconnaissance Badgers or Bears on the west coast of Africa. Unless Zemlya ran into the survivors at once, it could be a day or two before any mass search was laid on. By then, Uranus would be within forty-eight hours of Ponta de Calcanhar.

The day after the mutiny, Friday, 6 January, was therefore a 'twitch' day. Yanov, Reek's opposite number, was the first to pick up Zemlya's transmissions. She kept calling every half-hour and did not give up until 1800. An hour later she made a direct transmission in cipher to C-in-C, Black Sea.

From that moment onwards, the attitude of the mutineers changed. Until then, they had been elated by their apparent success. From now on, it was to be a race against time — and luck was what they most needed. Just before 2100, on the evening of the sixth, C-in-C, Black Sea began calling Uranus directly, demanding her position. The transmissions continued far into the morning of Saturday, 7 January. There was another interval for over an hour, and then the traffic between Zemlya and C-in-C, Black Sea became incessant. All was now in cipher.

The mutineers had agreed that Litke, Fomin and Salza should act as their elected executive committee; but it was Salza who first made known his anxieties during that same morning of the seventh. His fears were contagious and disagreement began to show among the mutineers.

The afternoon of 7 January brought matters to a head. Black Sea began calling again: this time, C-in-C was reporting in plain language that the motor cutter had been picked up. The transmission was repeated — that was all.

Then, in the early evening, Surov picked up through his binoculars the curious pinnacles of St Paul's Rocks which rear sixty feet above the surface of the mid-Atlantic.

By a vote of two to one (Salza against), it was decided to get rid of Grenz and the first lieutenant.

— Derek Warne

CHAPTER TWENTY-FIVE

Alexei Slepak was held under close arrest in his cabin for two days, allowed to see no one. He was treated brusquely, but was permitted, under escort, to the heads; his food was handed to him by the sentry through the door. Alexei had grown accustomed to the rhythmical beat of the diesels; in his judgement, *Uranus* had remained on her southerly course. Then, at about noon on the second day, 7 January, after a larger meal than usual, the door was flung open. Chief REA Litke stood before him, a sardonic grin twisting his pale face. He closed the door behind him; then, pistol in hand, he heaved himself onto Alexei's bunk, legs dangling over the edge.

'I apologize for not coming to see you before, sir,' he said, maintaining the courtesies. 'But I've been busy in the department seeing that there was no slip-up in the routines. The sentries have been treating you properly?'

Alexei remained standing. He was astonished at Litke's suavity. There had been senseless butchery, but Litke seemed now to have the mutineers tightly under his control.

'We've been discussing what's best to be done with our first lieutenant.' The leader of the mutineers sat grim-faced, dark eyes boring into Alexei. 'Our decision regarding Grenz was simple...' He grinned as he stroked the pistol in his hand. 'You know our commissar shot down young Istomin in cold blood, through the back of the head?'

'The sentry told me.'

'And Klavitter — he killed three of us. We don't know whether Rykov will live. Nakhimov is short of watchkeepers in the engine room. The executive committee wanted to dispose of you both.'

'Then why haven't you? You're a ruthless enough bastard.'

'Keep your cool, Slepak.' Alexei watched Litke's long fingers caressing the trigger guard of the gun. 'At first, I was all for eliminating you both — but I have a certain reluctance in dealing with you as we would like to deal with Grenz. Surov spoke up for you. He's no fool, your fourth hand.'

'A gutless traitor.'

'He's given you a chance. I had to put it to the vote, but the decision is the right one.'

'For God's sake, get on with it.'

'If Grenz and you can be found alive, our act of mercy — Grenz certainly deserves execution — might help us with the Brazilians. Politically, our clemency might affect their attitude when we ask for asylum.'

'You're bound for Brazil? You'll never get away with it.'

Litke ignored him, but he never lifted his eyes from his prisoner. 'Don't try and rush me, Slepak. The sentry outside has orders to shoot if you try anything.' He went on: 'We're setting you adrift in the dory, Grenz and you together.'

The vibration from the main engines was diminishing.

'Why are we easing down?' Alexei was peering through the scuttle.

'Surov sighted St Paul's Rocks twenty minutes ago,' Litke said. 'We're leaving you here.'

'In the dory?' Alexei snapped. 'That cockleshell? You're a bloody murderer, Litke. I often wondered about you: you're a treacherous bastard. I thought you, at least, would remain loyal.'

'You don't know anything about me, Slepak — of what I've suffered through the system. I love Russia, but I can't get out quickly enough. These are unusual methods, I admit. I've always admired unorthodoxy.'

'Leave me adrift in that dory? *Alone with Grenz?*' Alexei laughed bitterly. 'We don't stand a chance, and you know it.'

'You're not far off the shipping lanes. St Paul's Rocks are a landfall, Surov tells me. If only your bodies are found, it will be presumed that *Uranus* foundered.'

'And if we're never found? Not even our corpses?'

'*Uranus*'s disappearance will remain another mystery of the sea — okay by us, because we'll be scuttling her off Brazil. Either way, you lose, we win.' He laughed softly. 'Grenz is in the dory ... mustn't keep him waiting. I've organized food and water, and Salza's chucked in a few odds and ends. I'd be grateful if I were you, Slepak. He's unhappy at leaving you alive. I've even had to take his gun off him. He's an animal compared to Fomin.' Litke slipped from the bunk and jerked his pistol. 'We've always got along, Slepak, you and I,' he said. 'But if the others had had their way, you wouldn't be alive. Surov and I have given you a chance, even though it means being cast adrift in the open Atlantic with a madman like Grenz. Take anything you want with you.' Litke stood aside, watching Alexei gathering up his gear: binoculars, oilskin, seaman's knife, his precious diary in its sailcloth. Then he ripped a sheet from his bunk.

'What d'you want that for?'

'Might give us protection from the sun.' Alexei ignored the proffered hand; he stepped out into the wardroom flat, where the sentry prodded him up the ladder with the snout of his automatic.

They had lighted the dory alongside the port side, where Salza was tending the painter. A white-faced Surov was watching from the port wing, as Slepak passed between the silent sailors manning the upper deck. Slepak ignored Surov's salute. Without a word, he shinned down the ladder to the boat deck.

Bobbing alongside was the six-metre dory; Grenz was peering anxiously upwards, from where he sat awkwardly on the centre thwart. A jumble of gear filled the boat, which had changed its colour.

'Why's it grey now?' Slepak asked Litke, who was following closely behind him.

'We've scraped off the name. Sorry if the paint's still tacky. Get going, Slepak.'

In that second, Alexei was overwhelmed by a lunatic urge to rush Litke, to try to seize his gun, then hold him hostage. But one glance at Salza, his leathery face glowering with hate, was enough to convince Alexei that any attempt at turning the tables would be suicidal. He slung the binoculars around his neck, dropped the oilskins into the dory, secured his knife about his waist and scrambled over the gunwales. He grabbed the painter, felt the weight tauten, then slithered down it and into the bows of the boat. He stood astride, bearing off from *Uranus*'s side.

'Slip the dory!' Litke was shouting up to the bridge. 'Slow ahead.' The painter slatted at Alexei's feet; the ship's side began sliding past.

Alexei scrambled across Grenz and into the sternsheets. The dory bobbed in *Uranus*'s wash, then wallowed in the long swell. They sat in silence, staring at *Uranus*, until her smudge disappeared below the shimmering horizon.

CHAPTER TWENTY-SIX

'I hate your guts, Grenz,' Slepak said. 'You detest me. We can't carry on like this, if we're to survive.'

Grenz, who had sat staring moodily towards the southern horizon until long after *Uranus* had vanished, finally turned round. His face was puffy; blood had congealed across his cheek and his left eye was half-closed. 'What do you propose? I'm no seaman, Slepak.'

'Help me make this dory seaworthy. At least her hull's sound. We'll check on the gear; then we can decide what's best to be done.' Slepak wrapped the binoculars inside his oilskin and stuffed them carefully on top of his wrapped manuscript in the stern locker. He took off his tunic and placed it beside the oilskin. 'It'll be cold at night,' he said.

'It's bloody hot now,' Grenz grumbled, peeling off his own jacket. 'It's still only two o'clock and I burn easily.'

'We'll rig an awning, as soon as the boat's shipshape.'

For the next hour, Grenz co-operated. They sorted out the gear: one plastic container of drinking water; twelve packets of hardtack raisin biscuits; ten fathoms of three-centimetre rope; a tarpaulin about three metres square; a ball of twine; and three oars with a pair of metal crutches.

'It's about 1500,' Alexei said. 'We each have a wristwatch. Timekeeping will be vital if we are to write up a proper log. You can occupy yourself with that, Grenz.' Alexei extracted one of the pencils and a sheet of the precious paper from his wrapped package. '1500. Weather calm,' he said as he wrote, setting up the log for Grenz. 'Estimated position, vicinity of St

Paul's Rocks.' He glanced at Grenz. 'We'll assume Litke was not lying. Now, what's our best course?'

Grenz sat on the centre thwart, doing what he was told. He spoke rarely, offering no objections as he watched Alexei snugging down the boat.

'There's no reason for Litke to deceive us,' Alexei said. 'They may have wished you dead, Grenz, but they didn't kill you. Why?'

'We're more use to them alive — if we're picked up.'

'If we're close to St Paul's Rocks, we must be in the northern end of the south equatorial current which sets somewhere between north-west and south-west. I learned something during my morning watches.'

'How does that help us?' Grenz grumbled.

'There's no point in pulling against the current. If we set a westerly course, we'll have part of the current with us. We should steer towards the shipping lanes — Buenos Aires to Europe.'

There was no compass in the dory, but by watching the setting sun, they guessed their westerly heading. At 1730 they stowed the spare oar beneath the thwarts; they shipped the oars and Grenz began pulling from the centre thwart. They changed rounds at 1800, deciding upon half-hour tricks when under oars. They pulled for two hours, each wrapped in his own thoughts, while dusk fell like a mantle upon their empty world.

'That'll do for a bit,' Slepak said, with a half-smile. 'We'll rig some sort of sail tomorrow with the tarpaulin. We've enough rope for the sheets, as well as for rigging a jury mast.'

'I'm not used to this,' Grenz said. 'Bloody exhausted.'

So, their hands and backsides already blistered, they prepared for the night. They broached the plastic water can, using the lid as a pannikin. 'For how long should we ration ourselves, Grenz? Six packets of biscuits each and about ten litres of water. We'll fish if we can make a hook.'

'There's no line.' Grenz was a better commissar than a seaman. He sat glumly watching the sunset. 'Slepak,' he said suddenly. 'If we're picked up and returned to the Soviet Union, they'll deal with you as harshly as they will with me.'

Alexei was nibbling his half-biscuit. 'What are you implying?'

'You are as guilty as I am. We both failed to prevent this mutiny.'

'Don't be so bloody stupid,' Slepak retorted. 'You accepted looted property from a sailor — whether the stereo was sold or given to you by your informer, Richter, is irrelevant.'

Grenz was sitting erect, his fingers clutching the edge of the thwart.

'And after you'd murdered Istomin,' Alexei went on, 'by shooting him in the back, you didn't offer much resistance.'

'No more than you did, Slepak,' Grenz shouted in the vast emptiness. 'You were too bloody soft with them.' He was struggling to keep his cool.

'If they pick you up,' Alexei continued, 'they'll court-martial you; I'll see to that.'

'I'm sure you would, even after this.'

'Damn right I will,' Alexei blurted. 'And your activities with Richter didn't endear you to the troops.'

Grenz had risen from the thwarts and was leaning aft, his fists clenched. 'Don't speak like that again!' he blazed. 'I'll throttle you with my bare hands.'

Slepak sat rigid on the after thwarts. 'Yes, I believe you would!' He unwound his knife from his lanyard and flicked open the blade. He levelled the shining steel at Grenz's stomach.

'You, Slepak,' Grenz said, sitting down abruptly, 'you think I'll let you get away with it, if we're both rescued? I've been watching you since before you joined. The KGB have opened their files on you and your woman's family, the Lazarevs. Once I get you ashore, you don't think we'll ever let you reach Israel, do you?' He snorted in disgust. 'Your mail, your telephone calls, they've all been intercepted.'

'I'm not surprised, you bastard. You're assuming that we'll both be picked up, aren't you? If we're rescued, we'll *both* be for the bullet or Siberia — you know that well enough. I don't intend to return to our native land with you.'

'What d'you mean?'

'Only that you're a double-crossing fool: you know damn well that there's a chance for you, provided you're the only survivor. But, with me alongside you…' Slepak stuck his fingers against his temple, pressing the imaginary trigger. He jabbed his opened knife towards Grenz again. 'And if *I'm* alone in this boat when she's found — she surely will be, with all her built-in buoyancy — I'll stand a good chance of clearing myself.'

'What'll you do?' Grenz snapped.

'Defect with the others, if we're picked up by a South-American bound ship.'

'And then to Israel,' Grenz sneered, 'to have it off with your bird.' His dirty laugh sullied the peace of the fading twilight. 'And you can live happily ever after. You'd rat too, like the mutineers?'

'Perhaps… Anything to escape the system which you, Grenz, so admirably represent.' Alexei stood up in the sternsheets and pointed across the starboard bow. He shut his knife and tied its lanyard around him. 'I suggest we stop squabbling. Look, there's something there!' A black finger was rearing up against the line of the western horizon. Alexei wrenched his binoculars from the oilskin and felt Grenz's eyes upon him while he focused.

'That must be them: St Paul's Rocks. I read them up in "The Pilot": the highest of them white with bird-lime. They're about twenty metres high and stretch for two cables, rising sheer out of the Atlantic. Look, Grenz, amazing, aren't they?'

In the excitement of the moment, they thrust aside their enmity. 'We're being set towards them. Get out the oars.'

Alexei turned the boat round and began pulling away from the pinnacle of rock now looming in the gathering darkness. But after fifteen minutes the rock was still rearing high above them, nearer than before. He spun the dory round, allowing her to be carried towards the incredible phenomenon.

'Thank God the weather's calm. We'll be passing too close. Here, Grenz, back me up on the oars: push against my hands.'

It was now very dark and impossible to judge distance. The rocks swept nearer, looming higher with each minute that passed. The dory was in the grip of the current, which was setting them swiftly upon the Rocks of St Peter and St Paul. There was no choice but to try to slide between them.

'Let me have the oars!' Alexei yelled against the mounting roar of the breakers in the darkness. 'Bear off when you can, but *don't stand up*! I'll try to steer clear.'

The black pinnacles of rock, their summits white from the guano even in the darkness, bore down upon them. Alexei half-turned the boat round to see better over his shoulder. Even though it was very dark, he glimpsed a whitened, derelict, multi-legged metal structure leaning drunkenly upon the highest rock. Thousands of birds screamed above them in the darkness, drowning the crash of the swell breaking lazily upon the rocks.

The surface was boiling and seething about the dory. With a touch on either oar Alexei was guiding her through, when Grenz began yelling and pointing across the port bow.

A wall of breaking seas foamed directly ahead — Alexei could do nothing but hold on, as the boat was suddenly flung in every direction. The water seethed and hissed about them, leaping in confused spouts. They were swamped.

'Bail like hell!' Alexei shouted. 'Use your hands — *anything!*'

It was impossible to keep the boat bows-on: she was being swirled uncontrollably in circles. The water was halfway to the thwarts — she would founder unless she had sufficient buoyancy. The tanks were still intact; they might be able to right her, if she capsized.

Then she was out of it, the hissing of the seas diminishing as the current bore them to the north-west, away from the terror of the race. With cupped hands, they laboriously scooped the water from the dory; by the time the water level was down to the bottom boards, they were exhausted. They were soaked and the chill was eating through to their bones.

'What's the time, Grenz?'

'Ten-twenty.'

'Do you want to take the next trick? Two hours each this time, keeping a look-out.'

'What the hell *can* we do if we sight anything?'

'Not much — at least we'll know we're in a shipping lane. During the day, we'll pull up and down it, instead of across.'

'Okay. Where'll you sleep?'

'Up for'd,' Alexei said. From there he could keep an eye on Grenz. Stretched out under the thwarts, with his head in the eyes of the dory, he would feel the movement if Grenz tried anything. 'Call me at midnight, to even up the watches. I'll do from midnight till two. Funny, ain't it, Grenz? I'm actually looking forward to the sun tomorrow. Shake me if you sight anything.'

Grenz sat in the sternsheets, crouched over the tiller, his massive shoulders outlined above the heaving horizon. He remained silent, glaring morosely in front of him. His eyes wandered continually over Alexei, who was stretched out on the sodden bottom boards. Not a word passed between the two men, but each was reading the other's mind: neither would be the first to fall asleep. Surreptitiously, Alexei opened his knife, then slid it beneath his thigh.

The motion of the dory was lulling him to sleep. Grenz was yawning, his huge hands clenching the tiller. He had disclosed his mind and Alexei knew now what to expect. Sleep was the enemy: the moment when Alexei succumbed would be his last. He pinched himself time and time again, as the watch dragged on. The blurred outline that was Grenz merged with the sea, melted away, showed briefly against the dim horizon. Alexei must *not* fall asleep. Grenz, on his own, had a chance to live: together, they were both condemned.

He stretched his hand to the steel beneath his thigh. If Grenz attacked when Alexei lapsed momentarily into sleep, his fingers would clench about the knife.

They changed tricks at two-hourly intervals. For Alexei, it was that half-hour before dawn which was the most terrible: he remained crouched over the useless tiller, his leaden eyelids closing spasmodically. Grenz was outstretched in the eyes of the boat, but Alexei could not be sure whether he was feigning sleep. Grenz knew that Alexei would not murder him in cold blood, so he could afford to wait. Slepak would eventually be overcome by exhaustion.

Then dawn broke. For Alexei, the worst of that first night was over. The sun climbed above the horizon, its heat already drying out their sodden clothes. It was going to be hot.

They set up a jury mast with one of the oars; they rigged a line from bow to stern as a backbone for the sheet which they stretched across as an awning. During the day they lay in its shade, stretched out on the sodden bottom boards. By 1600 their thirst was acute, so they drank their second pannikin of water. They wanted no food and craved nothing but sleep. To keep awake, Alexei extracted his diary, which he brought up to date with the other pencil he had stuffed in the packet.

Grenz was watching him. 'What are you up to?'

'Writing up my diary. Makes interesting reading, looking back on these last few years.'

'You know that's forbidden, keeping a diary?'

'I imagine so. I didn't bother to ask your fraternity.'

'No wonder *Uranus* mutinied — a first lieutenant who deliberately ignores regulations.'

'Dry up,' Slepak snapped. 'We're in the middle of the Atlantic — and I want to write. You're supposed to be keeping a lookout. We've been adrift only thirty-three hours — and we're bang in the middle of the lanes.'

'You sound very confident — but the current is taking us nor'westward. We'll be out of the lanes soon.'

'Most of the South American traffic uses St Paul's Rocks as a halfway checkpoint. I want to be picked up, even if you don't. We've only enough water for about another three days, with the two of us.'

The heat beneath the sheet was stifling. The reflection from the sea's surface upon the grey aluminium of the hull was cooking the air inboard. The two men had stripped off their trousers; their skins were already burnt, but so far they had resisted the temptation of splashing sea-water over each other. Their thirst was already acute, driving them to the water canister. The dory drifted across the long swell, rising to the crests then sliding down into the troughs, as the ocean surged relentlessly onwards, to break upon the distant coast of the African, American or European continents.

'What've you written in your diary? Scurrilous anecdotes about all of us? Here, show it me.' Grenz held out his hand for the manuscript.

Alexei ignored him. He'd promised Katya he would persevere with his book: his last entry had been the day before the mutiny, so he needed to enter the recent details before his memory blurred. His pencil flickered across the pages as he brought his story up to date. It was difficult to explain that his fellow castaway would prefer to see Slepak dead — and not only because the food and water would last double the time.

It was now five o'clock on Sunday, 8 January — thirty-four hours since they were cast adrift. Alexei's lids flopped again, his mind wandering, craving oblivion. He felt his head slump; he shook himself, tried to focus upon the round face of his enemy — and, in that second, he glimpsed the gleam of triumph in Grenz's dark eyes, where he lay watching, biding his time, his gross body stretched across the thwarts. Slepak would succumb soon — and his head slumped again, his chin falling upon his chest. He jerked up his head, tried to focus again.

He was aware of a shadow stealing across his closed lids. He tried to open his eyes, then he was conscious of the listing of the dory... The shadow was looming down upon him — and, while he struggled for consciousness, he felt a pair of hands knotting about his throat. He kicked out with all his might.

'Give me that bloody book!'

Grenz had stumbled backwards, when Slepak thrashed out with his feet. He had grabbed the manuscript, but he was a jumble of flailing limbs where he had crashed backwards across the centre thwart. Slepak, who was still gasping from the pain about his windpipe, flicked open the blade of his knife. He leapt upon Grenz and fought with an animal ferocity to regain his precious manuscript.

'Give it back,' he gasped, 'or I'll slit your bloody throat.'

He was above Grenz, pinning him across the thwarts. Grenz doubled his leg, trying to knee Alexei. As Slepak flung away, he sent the plastic water container flying. The lid sprang off; the can rolled on its side into the sternsheets.

'The water,' Grenz gasped. 'You've knocked the can over.'

They sprang apart to save the precious liquid spilling into the bilges. Alexei scrabbled towards the canister to set it upright. Except for the dregs, it was empty. They slumped back onto the thwarts.

'Enough for one more ration!' Slepak yelled into the emptiness. 'Hope you're satisfied.' Half-demented, he hurled himself again upon Grenz, who fell backwards, striking his head on the thwarts. Alexei grabbed his manuscript from between the knees of the bow thwarts, where his half-stunned adversary had placed it.

'Get for'd and stay there, Grenz,' Slepak gasped. 'You've another hour until your 1800 trick. If I seem to be asleep, don't bank on it.' And then he spoke with deliberate emphasis. 'Try anything again and I'll kill you in self-defence.' Once more, Alexei levelled the blade of his seaman's knife at him. 'If the weather deteriorates,' he panted, 'we'll have to cut up the tarpaulin to keep out the seas. We can rig up one of the oars as a mast, and we'll use the rest of the tarpaulin as a sail. I'll run before the wind, if I have to.'

Slepak snugged down the boat as dusk fell upon the evening of their second day. They ate a biscuit each, finished the last drop of water, then settled down for the night.

Whether Alexei saw the light of the next dawn depended on his staying awake, he was convinced of that. For the second night running, he stretched himself out in the eyes of the boat, while Grenz took the watch. Slepak could not fight sleep much longer. If Grenz attacked him, it would be a fight for survival.

CHAPTER TWENTY-SEVEN

First light was stealing upon the grey waters of the gently heaving ocean. Hazily Alexei registered the beauty and calculated that this was Monday, 9 January, their third morning adrift in the dory. He was crouched across the jerking tiller, his chin cupped in one hand, his opened knife clutched in the other. He had tried desperately to keep awake by counting the hours since that morning, aeons ago, on the Saturday when he had woken in his bunk for the last time, a prisoner in his own ship.

Forty-seven hours he made it; forty-seven hours without sleep. Forty-seven hours, then the ordeal of the race in the lee of St Paul's Rocks; forty-odd hours since his battle with Grenz; forty-seven hours … and his head flopped again across the tiller.

His brain was refusing to function. Beneath the struggle of trying to remain awake the terror lurked, the realization that death was stalking him. Grenz, who had slept, was patiently biding his time, waiting to strike the moment that Alexei relaxed. Soon, the struggle would be over soon… The gentle motion of the dory was lulling him to sleep, the slap-slap of the water against the sides the only sound on this vast ocean… Sleep, blessed slumber, that would bring the solace of eternal peace. Though it was now light, his mind and body refused to work, drugged by tiredness and a desperate thirst. He never heard the soft scraping, never felt the shift in the dory's trim when Grenz crept aft.

Alexei registered first the shock of a blow across his wrist. He cried out with the pain, instinctively shielding his head with his other arm. He felt the knife spinning from his fingers as Grenz scrabbled for it; watched it bounce on the gunwale before it fell over the side. He struggled to his feet and thrust with all his strength as Grenz grappled him.

His adversary had him by the neck again, his massive bulk forcing Alexei against the stern board. Grenz was forcing him backwards, straining Alexei against the tiller. With his last ounce of strength, Slepak braced his muscles until he felt they would snap.

Grenz's foot was slithering upon the greasy hog. Alexei ducked to the right, giving way suddenly to his adversary's pressure. Grenz stumbled forwards, losing his balance, his shin striking the edge of the after thwart. His feet shot from under him. The boat lurched to starboard. Slepak butted him in the stomach with his head — and Grenz was overbalancing wildly over the starboard side of the dory.

The sudden shift of weight flipped the boat back to port and Alexei was almost catapulted into the water. He grabbed at the thwarts, then realized that he was alone in the boat.

Grenz was screaming obscenities from the water, spluttering for breath. His hair straggled across his eyes as he lunged for the side of the boat. First his right hand and then his left clamped across the starboard gunwale of the dory.

'Slepak, Slepak!' he pleaded hysterically. 'Help me back into the boat. Come on, Slepak, we can both see it out, if we keep our heads.' He was staring upwards, his round face distorted by terror. His abject pleading turned to wild and naked threats, as Slepak stood over him.

Grenz cocked his right foot across the gunwale. The boat heaved, listed suddenly. Then he was rocking the craft, rhythmically heaving her over until her gunwales were dangerously close to the water. Slepak was desperately trying to counterbalance, but, on the sixth roll, water swept over the gunwales.

'You rat,' Grenz roared triumphantly. 'I'll fix you, you and your woman's family!' He was heaving himself from the water as he bore down with all his weight upon the gunwale. The sea was pouring in, across the starboard bow. Then Grenz had succeeded in gripping the gunwale with the angle of his knee — he was half into the boat.

Alexei grabbed the oar that lay across the thwarts, grasping the loom with both hands. He lifted the oar, swinging it backwards behind his shoulders. With a scything motion he crashed it down, sweeping the length of the boat. Grenz's leg disappeared. Then, when Slepak saw the gross fingers clutching at the gunwales, something snapped in his mind: a red mist was swimming before his eyes. He was determined to live — no other instinct registered. Grenz was frothing threats and obscenities. And then, his world swirling about him, Slepak swung the oar high above his head.

CHAPTER TWENTY-EIGHT

COLLATOR'S NOTE 5

The manuscript runs out in a barely legible, pencilled scrawl. I have left it unaltered, exactly as I found it. It is curious that Slepak changed to the first person. Perhaps the merciful processes of Nature were anaesthetizing his demented mind.

— Derek Warne

I don't know how many days and nights have passed since that morning of 9 January — yes, Monday, 9 January. No water — ran out two days ago, five days after the storm — but there are three biscuits.

I could not write after that terrible morning. I left my diary until now: I can fight no longer. But I'll try to record the last details before I collapse. No hope now — death is so near, nothing matters — but someone may find ... this awful business... This is my true account.

Grenz was staring up at me, his hands gripping the gunwale. He was goading me to breaking-point. Gripping the loom, I swung the oar above my head; I crashed it down upon the fingers of his right hand. He screamed, his face distorted by horror and disbelief. The gap where his hand had been was a smear of skin, blood and fingernails. I lifted the oar again and smashed it upon his other hand. The oar splintered in two. He screamed again, dog-paddling in the water, less than a metre from the boat. He was yelling at me to stop, pleading with me to take him back on board.

My terror of him had driven me to a frenzy — it was him or me. With the half length of oar, I jabbed again and again with the splintered shaft. When the water-logged body finally rolled slowly over onto its chest, I tore down the other oar which we had lashed up as a jury mast.

I extracted the spare oar from the bottom boards, and with both oars I began pulling frenziedly — away, away from the body that was beginning to sink, barely buoyant as the air bubbled from his lungs and the sodden clothes.

I pulled and pulled until the corpse was no longer visible. And when I could struggle no further, I unshipped the oars. I hung over the side and vomited until I lost consciousness.

How long, I don't know — it was dark when I came to. Then a long, terrible night. Sleep for the first time in sixty hours — broken sleep — nightmares, terrifying flashes of the murder I had committed. My last glimpse of the body will be with me forever.

Next day, hot scorching sun; unbearable heat — I'm on fire; thirst, maddening thirst, 10 January. Terrible dreams — losing sanity. Night, haunted, awful night — gale got up. Rigged sail — ran before gale. Swamped.

Can't forget that hole that was his mouth — his eyes pleading ... but I was insane, crazed by terror and hate. I've gone mad. Mad...

Trying to make nor'west. No water — they'll never f-i-n-d m-e — m-a-d — Katenka, you mustn't — w-a-t-e-r — it's better... They'll never be a-ble — no — no — I d-o-n't —

Katenka, re-mem-ber Vir-g-i-n of Ka-za-n — al-ways —

EPILOGUE

That's how the manuscript ended. The scrawl became illegible, finally running out obliquely with a slash across the page. The insight to Slepak's character, his incredible perseverance and stamina, was demonstrated when I first unrolled the manuscript from its packet: Slepak had, in his last moments of lucidity, meticulously wrapped up his diary to ensure its safety. The bundle will remain always in my keeping.

The unidentified man (his name, Alexei Slepak, is a pseudonym) is still held in the American psychiatric hospital. They said originally that he would remain insane until the end of his days.

I have identified the Lazarevs. I think of the courageous parents now safely in Israel; of Katya, obstinately refusing to accompany them, until she is sure that all hope for Alexei has evaporated. She dares not ask for a visa to America to search for him. Someday, she prays, he will return to her, a spectre come alive. So she remains in the Soviet Union, waiting. She does not know of the man in the psychiatric ward. How *can* I tell her, without alerting 'Them'? And I want to thank her, too, for the help with her letters and the manuscript, help which she passed to me, at great risk, through the agency of her parents.

My thoughts flash back to the babbling madman we picked up that day in the grey-painted dory. The consul's last report stated that 'Slepak' was, under modern treatment, beginning to show signs of improvement — 'he might,' they said, 'even make a rapid and total recovery.'

I shall go and see him when next my ship puts in at Charleston. If I can judge the timing right, perhaps I can be instrumental in bringing Katya Lazarev and Alexei together again, to realize their dreams. But if I misjudge things and arouse interest inside the USSR, I will have condemned them to an interminable separation, a living death for both.

I have traced the Lazarevs to their Israel address. The key lies with them. Perhaps they can persuade Katya to join them, without alerting the authorities? If they succeed, I will have realized the ambition I have cherished for these long years. Then, if Alexei can join them direct from the States, I will be able to enjoy the remainder of my sea-going days in the vessel I now command, at peace in my mind.

— Derek Warne, Extra Master, Collator, SS *Timor Princess*, South Atlantic

A NOTE TO THE READER

Dear Reader,

If you have enjoyed the novel enough to leave a review on **Amazon** and **Goodreads**, then we would be truly grateful.

Sapere Books is an exciting new publisher of brilliant fiction and popular history.

To find out more about our latest releases and our monthly bargain books visit our website: **saperebooks.com**